FORBIDDEN PASSION

Dominic said her n̶a̶... as if he ca... didn't res... it was wro... hilarating ... known. She lifted her lip... in a kiss that began softly but soon became more intense.

Their mouths moved sensuously together as the kiss carried them away. He pressed her hips to his, and wild sensations sprang to life inside her—like an ember bursting into flame. . . .

Camilla's Conscience

Camilla's Conscience

by

Sandra Heath

A SIGNET BOOK

SIGNET
Published by the Penguin Group
Penguin Books USA Inc., 375 Hudson Street,
New York, New York 10014, U.S.A.
Penguin Books Ltd, 27 Wrights Lane,
London W8 5TZ, England
Penguin Books Australia Ltd, Ringwood,
Victoria, Australia
Penguin Books Canada Ltd, 10 Alcorn Avenue,
Toronto, Ontario, Canada M4V 3B2
Penguin Books (N.Z.) Ltd, 182–190 Wairau Road,
Auckland 10, New Zealand

Penguin Books Ltd, Registered Offices:
Harmondsworth, Middlesex, England

First published by Signet, an imprint of Dutton Signet,
a division of Penguin Books USA Inc.

First Printing, February, 1995
10 9 8 7 6 5 4 3 2 1

Chapter 1

It was the end of March 1814, and there was a grand ball at Carlton House. Two thousand guests thronged the Prince Regent's London residence to applaud peace in Europe, and to celebrate the betrothal of the prince's only child, Princess Charlotte, to the hereditary Prince of Orange. An air of excitement exuded the whole capital, for the coming summer would not only see a royal wedding, but also momentous visits by the Czar of Russia and the Emperor of Prussia.

The ball was an unbearable crush that soon proved too much for Lady Camilla Summerton. After nearly two years of self-imposed exile on her late husband's Gloucestershire estate, she'd lost her taste for the social whirl, and as soon as politeness allowed, she slipped away from the ballroom to seek a quiet corner. The jeweled circlet around her forehead felt uncomfortably tight, and she wished she'd chosen a lighter gown than the green velvet.

She had long dark hair, a creamy complexion, and expressive brown eyes, and at thirty-five her slender figure was the envy of many younger women. She was considered striking rather than beautiful, and as the daughter of the late Earl and Countess of Southwell was aristocratic to her fingertips, but she no longer felt at home among the *haut ton*. She'd only been in London for a week, staying at an elegant rented house in Cavendish Square, but was already chafing to return to the seclusion of Summerton Park.

Pausing at the bottom of the ballroom steps, she looked back at the glittering chamber. Memories flooded painfully over her. She'd met Harry on these steps fifteen years ago. How old it made her feel. And how lonely. Elizabeth had been right; leaving the country was a monumental error of judgment.

Gathering her skirts determinedly, she hurried away toward the nearest door, passing through anteroom after anteroom until at last there were hardly any guests to be seen. Her destination was a little-used music room at the end of the house, but as she reached the door she heard a playful giggle coming from beyond it. Lovers, she thought instinctively, but as she paused with her hand on the handle, someone called behind her.

"Camilla! I've been looking everywhere for you."

The woman who'd addressed her was Lady Elizabeth Oxforth, the friend who'd wisely advised her against coming to town again. Camilla turned and smiled. "It seems you've found me, Elizabeth." As she spoke, she couldn't help but be conscious of the dismayed silence that suddenly descended over the music room. Evidently those inside went in fear of imminent discovery.

Elizabeth hurried over in a flurry of purple taffeta. There were plumes springing from her honey-colored hair, and she shimmered with diamonds. For a long time she'd reigned supreme as the unchallenged belle of London society, but had become a little rounded over the past year or so. "Are you enjoying tonight?" she asked as she reached Camilla.

Honesty was the best policy. "Actually no, it's a horrid press and full of far too many memories. I wish I'd never left Summerton Park."

"I did warn you, although it escapes me how anyone can be so happy buried away in the wilds of the country, especially in a house that is more oriental temple than anything else."

"I loathe people who say 'I told you so,' and as to Summerton Park being an oriental temple"—Camilla smiled—"well, I suppose I have to concede that point as well."

"You can't deny it. I vow a Peking mandarin would feel quite at home in that neck of Gloucestershire."

"Perhaps he would, but so do I."

Elizabeth smoothed her long white gloves and changed the subject. "There was a time when you'd have positively reveled in an occasion like tonight."

Camilla drew a long breath. "I know, I just didn't think it would be so hollow without Harry."

"Ah, yes. Harry." Elizabeth lowered her glance for a moment, but then went on more briskly. "Well, in spite of your wretchedness about being here, I have to compliment you on your togs and coiffure. You look very elegant and fetching, if a little pale."

"I may have dressed elegantly tonight, but I certainly haven't dressed wisely. It was very silly to wear this green velvet, and as for a circlet . . . !" Camilla flicked open her fan and employed it for a moment. There was still a very intriguing silence from behind the door. She knew the room. It was part of a small single-story wing built on to the rear of the house and was lit by a colored glass lantern roof that couldn't be opened, which meant that whoever was inside couldn't leave except by the door.

Elizabeth didn't notice her interest in the room. "How do you keep your figure so trim? I believe I loathe you, you wretch. There's far too much of me these days, but I daresay it's the price of having children."

"How are the boys?"

"Gaining notoriety at Eton. Eton already, it makes me feel like Methuselah." Elizabeth sighed. "How I long for those halcyon days of yore when I was Lady Elizabeth de Marne, the belle of three successive seasons. It was so wonderful to be pursued by every eligible gentleman in London."

"As I recall, you were quite adept at doing the pursuing yourself, indeed it's a pastime you've continued all through your married life," Camilla reminded her.

Elizabeth smiled a little wickedly. "One has to do something when one's husband is more devoted to the green baize than his wife. George and I have a very sensible marriage—we only turn to each other in bed when there's nothing better to do."

"You're far too cruel about George." Camilla smiled. "By the way, I hear William is betrothed."

"Ah, yes, little brother William."

"Little? He's all of twenty-five!" Camilla declared, thinking of charming Lord de Marne, heir of the earldom of Highnam.

"Yes, he's twenty-five, but behaves as if he's ten years younger," Elizabeth replied. "This betrothal to Lord Penshill's daughter has been planned for several years now, but suddenly William is the original reluctant groom. He had to be positively threatened before he'd go through with it, and to say he's a sulky bear over it is putting it mildly. I don't know what's the matter with him. It isn't even as if Alice Penshill is drab; on the contrary, she's as pretty as a picture, as William himself was obliged to concede on the only occasion he's been persuaded to actually meet her!"

"They've only met once?" Camilla was taken aback.

Elizabeth nodded. "Yes, with parents present throughout and therefore no chance at all to get to know each other. William was offhand about everything, and hasn't improved since. Truth to tell, Father has now become so incensed he's threatening to disinherit him unless he toes the line from now on."

"Disinherit him? That's a little extreme, isn't it?"

"Father and Lord Penshill are old friends, and both are set on an alliance. Father swears he'll make one of my cousins the next Earl of Highnam if William doesn't buck up." Elizabeth paused. "I suppose you've heard there's a marquessate in the offing?"

"There have been whispers," Camilla confirmed.

"Father's been tipped the wink that provided no hint of scandal adheres to the family name between now and then, he'll be the Marquess of Highnam come Christmas. As you can imagine, he's pawing the ground with impatience, for this is something he's been wanting for as long as I can remember. I hope William doesn't upset the applecart by causing a stir of any sort over this match, because if it hinders this wretched marquessate in any way, Father's quite capable of throwing him out. I love my brother very much, but his behavior of late has been quite appalling. Oh, let's change the subject, for the whole business has brought me quite low." Elizabeth studied her. "Has any gentleman caught your eye since you came to town?"

"No."

"No one at all?"

"No."

"Harry's been gone for virtually two years now. When was it? June 1812? Good heavens, it's long since time you considered taking another husband."

"I don't want another husband."

"Then borrow someone else's," Elizabeth urged with her customary lack of scruple.

"I've never done that before, and I don't intend to start now! You're completely unprincipled."

"I know, but it's great fun. You should try it. By the way, Dominic's here tonight, did you know?"

Camilla looked away. "No, I didn't, nor am I interested."

"Naturally I didn't speak to him, we merely looked through each other."

"The Earl of Ennismount is the most despicable man in Britain." Camilla's tone was cordial, but her eyes shone with loathing as she spoke of the man who'd been Harry's closest friend.

Elizabeth eyed her. "So you still blame him as much as ever for Harry's death?"

"Yes. Dominic should never have provoked Harry into buying that brute of a horse in the first place."

Elizabeth shifted uncomfortably. "I know, but it has to be said that dear as Harry was, there were times when he could be the most hotheaded, stubborn, and determined fellow in creation."

"Dominic knew Harry wasn't up to such a difficult animal. He could and should have stopped him riding it, especially in a violent thunderstorm when the horse was distressed anyway!"

"Dominic insists there was nothing he could do."

"There had to be *something* he could do, if only call for help to forcibly restrain Harry. I'd have stopped the ride if I'd have been there, but I didn't arrive back in time." Camilla looked away, for it was always painful to mention that terrible day. She would never believe Dominic's version of events. Never.

"Can I ask you a very personal question?"

"How personal?" Camilla inquired.

"Exceedingly. It's this—was Dominic ever your lover?"

Camilla's breath caught, the color rushed hotly into her cheeks. "Certainly not!"

"Forgive me for asking, but there was always such a charged atmosphere between you that I thought—"

"You're wrong," Camilla replied firmly.

"Yes, I can see I am." Camilla looked very uncomfortable. "Don't be angry with me for asking, it's just that seeing him again tonight brought it all back a little. You see, at the time I was absolutely convinced you and he were more to each other than mere friends." She gave a nervous laugh. "That will teach me to judge others by my own abysmal standards, will it not?"

Camilla's silence was very telling of her opinion of her friend's standards.

Elizabeth went on more briskly. "Actually, I'm told he's in a sour mood tonight, but then I suppose that's nothing unusual these days." She adjusted her plumes. "It seems he's not well pleased with the latest political duty heaped on him by Prinny and the prime minister. They've chosen Ennismount House to take care of a young lady, Czar Alexander's ward or some such thing. Dominic is regarded as a suitable protector, and his aunt, Lady Cayne, is the chaperone. The young lady has been brought to London from school in Bath in time to meet the czar's sister, the Grand Duchess Catherine, when she arrives in a day or so."

"I didn't even know one of the czar's wards was in England," Camilla said.

"Nor did I, and if she's in Lady Cayne's tender care, no doubt she wishes she was still in Bath."

Camilla pulled a face. Lady Cayne was one of the most redoubtable matrons in London. She'd once been lady-in-waiting to Queen Charlotte, and believed rules were made to observe to the final letter, with no allowance for inexperience.

Elizabeth grinned. "I'm told the young woman is proving quite a handful, with far too many airs and graces. A proper little St. Petersburg saucebox."

Camilla glanced toward the adjoining anteroom and saw Elizabeth's husband. "I believe George is looking for you," she warned.

"Oh, no!"

"If you go that way . . ." Camilla nodded toward another door.

Gathering her purple taffeta skirts, Elizabeth hurried away.

Camilla sighed with relief. Elizabeth always meant well, but could be aggravating at times, especially when she insisted on dragging Dominic's name into things.

George spotted her and approached with a broad smile on his amiable face. "Why, Camilla, how excellent it is to see you in these surroundings again." He wasn't by any means a handsome man, but his warm character won him many friends. He had gray eyes and his brown hair was sparse on top, so that his bald patch shone as he bowed over her hand.

She'd always liked him and was sorry he had so much to put up with from Elizabeth. But he loved his unfaithful wife, and seemed prepared to tolerate her indiscretions, although whether or not such forbearance would continue forever remained a matter of conjecture. Camilla always suspected that sooner or later the last straw would be reached, and Elizabeth would rue her inconstancy. In him she had a treasure of a husband, but it seemed she couldn't appreciate his worth. For the moment, however, he was still in a mood to grin and bear it. "You're looking very well, George," she said.

"And so are you. I'm more than glad to see you out of mourning at last."

She lowered her eyes, for she knew he'd never thought highly of Harry. He'd tried not to show it, but couldn't really fool her. There had always been a little friction between the two men, nothing to put one's finger on, and certainly nothing to cause out-and-out awkwardness, but it had been there all the same.

She remembered noticing him at Harry's funeral. His expression had been very eloquent as the coffin had been taken into the Summerton family vault. If he'd said good riddance out loud, his feelings could not have been more clear. But she didn't resent him for it; how could she when she knew full well that Harry's expression would have been exactly the same if it had been Sir George Oxforth's interment!

George glanced around in puzzlement. "I could have sworn I saw Elizabeth with you a moment ago.

At least, I saw someone in a gown of the same shade of purple as hers."

Camilla felt uncomfortable. "Er, yes, she was with me. You've missed her by a whisker. She went that way if you really wish to find her."

He smiled ruefully. "To be truthful, I only wanted to tell her I'm going now. Prinny's in a God-awful grumpy mood because Princess Charlotte's in a sulk about something the Prince of Orange did— or didn't do, I'm not quite sure which—and for the past two hours I've listened to him complaining. On top of that it's such an abominable crush here that I've developed a fancy for a few quiet hours at Brooks' Club. That is if anyone remains to enjoy a few hands of cards, since I think the world and his wife is crammed in here tonight."

"What humbug, sir," Camilla replied teasingly. "The green baize is the be-all and end-all of your existence, and even if it hadn't been a crush here tonight, and the prince hadn't spent the last two hours grumbling, you'd still be hankering to go to Brooks's."

He grinned. "I fear you're right, I'm a slave to the gaming table. Now then, which way did you say Elizabeth went?"

"That way, but if all you wish to do is tell her you're leaving, why don't you ask a footman to pass your message on?"

"What a capital notion." He beamed at her and kissed her hand again. "I'll love you and leave you, my dear. *Au revoir.*"

"*Au revoir,* George."

Camilla waited until he'd gone and then drew a long breath as she turned to look at the music room door, beyond which all was still silent. But she knew two people were there, and she was filled with curiosity as to who they might be.

Without warning, she opened the door and went in.

Chapter 2

The music room was candlelit, and the soft glow swayed over a golden harp and beautiful inlaid clavichord. There was a pink brocade sofa against one wall, and on it sat a young girl of about seventeen. She was petite, with golden hair and large lilac eyes, and wore a yellow silk gown that she fiddled nervously with as she endeavored to appear composed and natural.

There was no sign of anyone else, but the lack of any window or other door meant the second person, the young woman's lover, had to be hiding somewhere, and there was only one suitable place—behind the sofa.

Camilla affected to be surprised to find the room occupied. "Oh, I'm sorry, I didn't realize anyone was here."

"That is quite all right, *madame*," the girl replied. She had a French accent, but there was nothing French in her appearance. Nor was there anything English, except perhaps for her clothes, which were recognizably the work of a very superior London couturiere.

Camilla wondered who she was. Whatever her

name, however, one thing was certain—she was far too young to be conducting a liaison of any kind, or to be unchaperoned at an occasion like this. Had she given some poor matron the slip? Determined to find out more, Camilla sat down on the sofa. "I don't believe we've met before. I'm Lady Camilla Summerton," she said.

"I—I am Sophie Arenburg," the girl replied with barely disguised dismay. The last thing she wanted right now was a cozy chat!

Arenburg? The name conveyed nothing to Camilla. "This must be one of your first balls, mademoiselle."

"It is." Sophie lowered her glance. Her unease was almost palpable, as well it might be when she clearly dreaded being found out in an assignation. She managed a smile. "I—I am here at the invitation of the Prince Regent. I am the ward of Czar Alexander of Russia, and have come to London from school in Bath to be presented to the czar's sister, the Grand Duchess Catherine, when she arrives in a few days' time."

Camilla's eyes cleared then. The difficult young lady Dominic and his aunt had charge of! Well, that explained the French accent, for the Russian court spoke only French. "I, er, believe I've heard of you, mademoiselle."

"Yes?" Sophie's response was surprised, but they both knew Elizabeth's words had been plainly audible through the door.

"You say you were in school in Bath?" Camilla went on.

"*Oui,* at Miss Simmonds' Academy. I was there for three years. The czar heard such excellent reports of Miss Simmonds that he invited her to teach me in St. Petersburg, but she would not leave England. So I was sent here instead." This last was said with more than a touch of resentment.

The czar's ward was clearly an exceedingly proud and spirited young woman who had rightly been described as difficult, Camilla thought, pondering the prodigious stir recent goings-on in this very room could cause. The czar's formidable sister was about to descend on the capital, and her fury could only be imagined if she learned how Mlle Arenburg had been permitted to get into such a compromising situation beneath the Prince Regent's very roof. The prince himself would be horrified, and as for Dominic and Lady Cayne, their dereliction of duty beggared belief. On the very eve of the grand duchess's arrival, and with Alexander himself expected in June, how could they have been so remiss as to allow their charge to wander about unchaperoned?

But while these dire thoughts were passing through Camilla's head, Sophie was still thinking about the much more mundane matter of the school in Bath. "I did not like Miss Simmonds," she murmured.

Camilla smiled. "She can be quite a dragon," she agreed.

"You know her?"

"I was once at the same academy."

"I'm glad I do not have to go back there again, for she treated me like a small child and said I was too naughty."

Camilla didn't reply, for her experience so far of Sophie Arenburg suggested the headmistress was probably justified.

Sophie smiled then. "I like London, though, even if it does mean having to stay at Ennismount House."

"Ah, yes, I understand Lord Ennismount and Lady Cayne are in charge of you at present."

Sophie pulled a face. "Yes."

"Perhaps you should be with them now, instead of being in here on your own?"

Sophie shifted her position slightly. "Yes, I suppose so, but I do not like them. They are both so—so *stuffy*—and Lord Ennismount behaves as if he is as old as his aunt."

Camilla hid her amusement, for it was true, although there had been a time when Dominic had been the very opposite. She could remember the early days, when he'd been renowned for his roguish sense of humor, his dashing gallantry, and his willingness to flout any convention. Not now, however. Oh, certainly not now.

At that moment there was a slight scuffling behind the sofa, and Sophie showed great presence of mind by immediately pretending to sneeze. "Oh, *pardon, madame*," she said, searching for a handkerchief in her spangled reticule.

Camilla affected not to notice anything odd. "It's a little cool in here, and since we've already agreed you should go back to Lord Ennismount and Lady Cayne, perhaps we should leave now." She got up purposefully.

But before Sophie had time to follow suit, the door opened and none other than Dominic himself came in.

Sophie's face fell. "Lord Ennismount!"

"Mademoiselle," he replied tersely, according her a brief but courteous bow. The fifth Earl of Ennismount was tall and coldly handsome, with penetrating blue eyes and thick coal-black hair that he always wore just a little longer than fashion dictated. At nearly forty, he was acknowledged to be not only one of London's most handsome lords but also one of its most eligible, and it was well known that the betting book at White's contained numerous wagers as to when and who he would eventually marry. But these days his name was so rarely associated with any suitable lady that it was beginning to be felt he would remain unwed.

Camilla had stiffened defensively the moment he entered. The past, already so close tonight, was suddenly almost tangible. Her heartbeats quickened as conflicting emotions tumbled almost uncontrollably through her. They were the old emotions that had beset her almost from the very beginning where he was concerned, and the years hadn't blunted their edge. He affected her as much now as he had when she was only twenty. It was as if he wielded some immense power and was able to reach into her soul no matter how far apart they were. Elizabeth was so right. There *had* always been an atmosphere between them. But they'd never been lovers, never true lovers . . .

He was equally as startled to see her, and after a moment's hesitation gave her a cool bow. "Good evening, Lady Camilla," he murmured, before returning his rather irritated attention to Sophie. "Mademoiselle, your absence has been noted, and we've been searching everywhere for you. You should not have left Lady Cayne without permission."

Sophie's chin came up mutinously. "I do not have to tell you everything I do," she declared.

"Yes, you do, Mademoiselle Arenburg. I like the situation as little as you, but the Prince Regent and the prime minister have decided my aunt and I shall have custody of you until the grand duchess arrives. That means we are responsible for you, and you are answerable to us, so the very least you can do is conduct yourself correctly. You should certainly accord my aunt the respect she is due."

Sophie had the grace to look a little contrite. "I am sorry, *milord,* but I—I had a headache and came in here to be a little quiet."

On the spur of the moment Camilla decided to back her up. "Yes, it's true, sir. She told me she felt unwell, and I accompanied her here."

Sophie was startled, and Dominic pursed his lips disbelievingly. "Did you indeed?" he murmured.

"Yes, I did indeed, sir." When he spoke in that patronizing tone, Camilla would have supported even Old Nick against him.

"Well, if you've been with her, it's clear she cannot have come to any harm, Lady Camilla." He held her gaze for a moment, and then returned his attention to Sophie. "Please return to Lady Cayne, mademoiselle."

"*Oui, milord,*" Sophie replied obediently. She glanced at Camilla. "Thank you so much for taking care of me, my lady."

"It was nothing, mademoiselle," Camilla replied, deliberately looking at the sofa so the girl realized the gentleman's hidden presence had been known all along.

Sophie gasped. "I—I will go to Lady Cayne now, *milord,*" she said swiftly, then gathered her skirts to flee the room.

Dominic lingered. "Lady Camilla, do you still insist you've been with her all along?" he asked bluntly.

"Of course."

"Yes, for no doubt you'd do anything you thought would confound me, wouldn't you?"

"You flatter yourself, sirrah."

"No, madam, I merely speak the truth." He searched her cold face. "How long ago now the old days, hmm? How far away those countless hours of close and happy friendship?"

"My lord I find it distasteful in the extreme that you, of all men, should attempt to remind me of how it once was."

He smiled thinly. "Yes, I'm sure you do, for guilty conscience is a dreadful thing."

She colored. "That is something of which you'd know a great deal, sir."

"Possibly, but it is also something with which you are personally acquainted, madam." Inclining his head, he followed Sophie from the room.

For a long moment Camilla could neither speak nor move, but at last she turned slowly toward the sofa.

"You can come out now, sir, whoever you are," she said.

There wasn't a sound from behind the sofa, and so she spoke again. "Sirrah, if you do not come out, I shall raise the alarm."

Someone began to move then, and very slowly a sheepish young gentleman emerged. Camilla stared, for it was Elizabeth's newly betrothed brother, William, Lord de Marne, the future Earl of Highnam.

"William?" She gasped.

He was of medium height, with a shock of chestnut curls and wide green eyes, and he avoided her startled gaze by making much of brushing some dust from his elegant evening clothes.

"Have you taken leave of your senses?" she asked. "You're engaged to Lord Penshill's daughter!"

He looked at her at last. "Maybe so, but I don't wish to be."

"Nevertheless, you are! How *could* you be so foolish as to make advances to Mlle Arenburg?"

He pressed his lips together and looked guiltily at the floor.

"William, you must stop this immediately. Mlle Arenburg is the czar's ward."

"I love her, and she loves me."

"William, she's only seventeen."

"Seventeen and three months exactly."

"And the three months makes the difference, I suppose." Camilla replied dryly. Then she gave him a cross look. "You, on the other hand, are old enough to know better. Apart from anything else, I understand your father's threatening to disinherit you unless you do right by the Penshill match."

"Only because he has a fancy to be a marquess," William replied savagely.

"And because he and Lord Penshill are old friends."

"My sister shouldn't have told you all this. Sophie and I could hear everything she said."

"Elizabeth and I go back a long way, and we're still good friends, even though I've been out of town for some time. If she were to find out about his—"

"What would Elizabeth know of love?" he cried softly. "She's too profligate for heartfelt emotion! I doubt she can even count the number of lovers she's had. I, on the other hand, love Sophie, I mean really love her!"

"And you imagine such fine sentiments will persuade the czar to give his ward to you? You're in Cloud-Cuckoo-Land if that's what you hope. Pursue this affair and you'll be penniless, for your father won't finance you if you ruin his chance of becoming a marquess, or if you turn down the Penshill match." Camilla sat down, and tapped her closed fan in her palm. "I covered for you a moment ago, which is more than you deserve. Your conduct is reprehensible in the extreme. Have you any idea of the furor this will cause if it gets out? The czar's sister is expected here at any moment, and the czar himself arrives in June, the last thing the Prince Regent and the government want is a scandal involving Mlle Arenburg!"

"But Sophie and I are deeply and truly in love, Camilla," William protested urgently.

"I seem to recall that during one of your many visits to Summerton Park, you once said the same thing about my gamekeeper's daughter," Camilla retorted a little unfairly, for he'd been fifteen at the time.

"I was a child then! This is hardly the same thing!" William replied indignantly.

"William, you're always head over heels in love with someone. You're sighing over a new sweetheart each time I see you, so why should I accept this as different?"

"Because it is."

Camilla's fan continued to tap, and then she sighed. "So you keep saying, but I'm afraid the reality of the thing is less romantic. There's far too much at stake here, so you must stop this affair immediately."

"Camilla—"

"Immediately, William." Camilla drew a long breath. "I want you to promise me you won't see Mlle Arenburg again."

"Would you have stopped seeing your late husband?" William challenged defiantly.

"That was different, Harry and I were free to marry each other."

"But—"

"It's no good arguing, William. You're in the wrong, and nothing will make it right. It's out of the question you should pay court to anyone other than Alice Penshill, and it's even more out of the question you should think of pursuing Czar Alexander's ward when the Grand Duchess Catherine is about to arrive in London. The international repercussions could be dreadful, as even I can see."

William gave an ironic laugh. "Ah, yes, the international repercussions."

Camilla caught an inflection in his tone. "Is there something you're not telling me, William?"

"No." He met her eyes.

"Then that is the end of the matter. You must forget Sophie Arenburg."

"It's damnably unfair," he muttered.

"No doubt, but I trust you see I'm right?"

For a moment he looked stubborn, but then nodded.

"And you promise not to see her again?"

"Yes."

"Good." Camilla got up. "Shall we rejoin the ball?"

Summoning the vestiges of good grace, he offered her his arm, and together they left the music room. But as they emerged they found Dominic waiting, and the dark look on his face was ample warning that he knew he'd been misled earlier.

Chapter 3

Acute embarrassment swept over Camilla as she realized he'd guessed she'd been less than honest with him.

William was dismayed. "Oh, lord . . ." he muttered under his breath.

Dominic advanced. "I thought as much," he breathed, giving William a furious look. "I'll have words with you in due course, sir, but for the moment I suggest you make yourself scarce, before I forget my manners and give you the physical drubbing you deserve as well as the verbal one you're going to get!"

"Lord Ennismount, I—"

"I trust I don't have to remind you it's in everyone's interest to keep this unfortunate business quiet, not least your own, unless you wish your father to find out. Now get out of my sight, and stay away from a certain young lady, or it will be the worst for you!"

Without further ado, William hurried away in the direction of the ballroom.

Camilla made to follow, but Dominic caught her arm. "Not so fast, madam, for I haven't finished with you yet." He steered her back into the music room and closed the door. "Your conduct tonight has been questionable in the extreme, Lady Camilla. It seems the two years you spent cooling your heels in the country have affected your judgment."

"How dare you!"

"No, madam, how dare *you!*" He replied acidly. "It ill becomes you to connive at an illicit affair between a seventeen-year-old girl and a fool like de Marne!"

"*Connive?* I haven't *connived* at anything," she fired back, loathing him so much that she could hardly refrain from striking him. Her indignation wasn't made any better by knowing he was right, for she had indeed connived. To a certain extent, anyway.

"Then how would you describe your actions?" he challenged, his blue eyes as hard as flint. "You *knew* Mlle Arenburg was meeting de Marne in that room, and you lied to me to protect them both. I find that totally unacceptable behavior."

"How can you, of all men, preach to *me* about unacceptable behavior?"

"My, how assiduously you cling to old imagined grudges," he breathed.

"I imagine nothing where you're concerned, sirrah," she replied softly, the last word uttered almost in a hiss.

"And I'm under no illusions about the sweetness of your nature either, madam, or about your incredible ability to remember only half the truth when it suits you. But we're wandering somewhat off course here, for we were talking of Mlle Arenburg. Maybe you refuse to admit that by assisting in any way in her dealings with de Marne you've been at best ill-advised, at worst downright lacking in principle, but perhaps you can be persuaded that you've been acting against the national interest."

Camilla blinked. "Because she is the czar's ward? Oh, come now—"

But he interrupted. "Yes, she's the czar's ward, but she's also about to be betrothed to Prince Ludwig of Prussia, nephew of King Frederick."

Camilla was aghast.

"So neither de Marne nor Mlle Arenburg chose to mention this to you?" he went on.

"No." She was shaken. So that was what William had nearly spoken of when she'd mentioned international repercussions! It was too much of the young lovers. Not only was William already betrothed, but Sophie knew her own future had been mapped out as well.

Dominic saw how stunned she was. "The official betrothal between Prince Ludwig and Mlle Arenburg is to take place here in London when the czar and King Frederick arrive in June, but the prince will be here in a day or so with the Grand Duchess Catherine. The grand duchess is the force behind the match, it's entirely her idea, and her word is law with the czar, who dotes on her to an extraordinary extent. Offend her and you offend Russia itself."

"I—I understand that, sir, but confess to being a little surprised that a mere mademoiselle, albeit one who is the czar's ward, should warrant such a lofty match."

He hesitated. "I know the reason, Lady Camilla, but cannot tell you."

"By which you mean you don't trust me?"

"By which I mean it's better I don't say anything."

Camilla studied him. "Then I will draw my own conclusion. Putting two and two together, I suspect Mlle Arenburg of being rather more than just the czar's ward, in fact I hazard to guess she might be his daughter, albeit on the wrong side of the blanket."

Dominic didn't comment.

She raised an eyebrow. "So I'm correct. Well, that would certainly explain the imperial family's interest in her, especially as the czar as yet has no legitimate children." She paused, her eyebrow still raised as she waited for him to answer.

"Madam, if you think I'm about to confirm or deny anything you've just said, you'll have a very long wait."

"Everything about you confirms what I've just said," she replied. "Besides, she has the look of the Romanovs, and is haughty enough to be one when she chooses." Camilla thought for a moment. "She obviously doesn't know who her father is," she said then.

"What prompts that comment?"

"Sir, if Mlle Arenburg knew Czar Alexander was her father, she'd be unbearably imperious."

"As the Grand Duchess Catherine already is," he observed. "She's opinionated, mischievous, meddling, and much given to intrigue, and our government doesn't in the least relish her presence here. It's through intrigue that she happened upon Ludwig. He's a minor princeling who frittered away his fortune and is in need of a suitable wife. The grand duchess decided he was the very husband Mlle Arenburg requires, and told the czar as much. Alexander promptly promised a huge dowry with the bride, and Ludwig pronounced himself prepared to overlook her lack of title."

"Her illegitimacy, you mean," Camilla corrected astutely.

"Her lack of a title," Dominic insisted. "Now the

grand duchess has further decided the official betrothal must take place here in London in June, when the presence of both the czar and King Frederick will give the match an unparalleled seal of royal approval."

"That cannot be denied."

"But although Catherine is eager for this match, there is another which she is suspected of wanting to wreck," Dominic went on.

"What match is that?"

"That between Princess Charlotte and the Prince of Orange. Russia doesn't approve for a variety of political reasons with which I won't bore you."

"But the match has already been formally recognized. It's one of the things we're celebrating here tonight, for heaven's sake!"

"That won't stop someone like the Grand Duchess Catherine. Everyone knows Princess Charlotte has reservations about marrying the Prince of Orange and that she doesn't get on with her father. That's fertile ground for an intrigante like the czar's sister, who comes here with a predisposition to dislike all things British, especially the royal family. Those in the know fear she has every intention of stirring up as much trouble as she can with Princess Charlotte. Therefore, bearing all this in mind, everything must be done to placate the grand duchess and keep her sweet while she's here. This can best be achieved by giving her a very full social calendar, and also doing everything possible to accord Mlle Arenburg's Prussian match every respect and importance, the plan being to keep Catherine too busy to have time to interfere in things that don't concern her. The plan was well on course—until tonight."

The pointed way this last was said provoked Camilla into indignation. "Are you accusing me of demolishing everything simply by spending a few minutes with the prospective bride?" she cried.

"No, I'm merely pointing out the delicacy of the situation now that de Marne is on the scene." He drew a long breath. "I've probably been very indiscreet telling you so much, but I feel it's important you understand the possible ramifications should events erupt into a full-scale scandal. If the Prussian match founders in any way because of what's happened here tonight, you may bet your last farthing that the grand duchess will scream from the rooftops that the Prince Regent, the British government, and everyone else here has been gravely lacking for permitting such misconduct."

Camilla looked at him a little mockingly. "And I daresay she'd be right," she murmured.

A little dull color entered his cheeks. "I must ask you again to remember that everything you've been told is *very* restricted information."

"I know when to hold my tongue and when not to, sir," she replied stiffly.

He gave a ghost of a smile. "Oh, yes, my lady, I know how, er, discreet you can be when it serves your purpose."

"That was uncalled for!"

"Was it? I think not. But we wander from the point yet again. Have I convinced you about how vital it is to keep Mlle Arenburg and de Marne apart?"

"You've made your point very lucidly indeed, sir. I admit to having been a little unwise earlier on, but assure you I didn't have any knowledge of the affair until I happened accidently on the tryst in this very room. However, it may interest you to know that William has already agreed to end the affair."

"Oh, you may count upon it being at an end, madam, for by the time I've finished with him, de Marne is going to wish he'd never even heard the name Arenburg."

"How diplomatic, to be sure," she murmured, beginning to feel for the unfortunate young lovers, even thought they'd been less than forthcoming with her. "Well, Lord Ennismount, since you are trusted in high places with such a delicate responsibility until the grand duchess arrives to take over, I'm sure your vast reserves of tact, discretion, and sensitivity will equip you handsomely for the ticklish task of telling Mlle Arenburg she's forbidden to see William again. I daresay you'll be so caring and sympathetic she won't shed even a single tear."

"Your tongue hasn't lost its edge, madam," he remarked.

"Unlike your honor," she replied in a tone that dripped vitriol.

"And what of *your* honor, my lady? You do remember once possessing such a thing, don't you?"

"I'm sure I recall it much more clearly than you do, sir," she replied coolly.

"I doubt it."

"If honor counts so very much with you, I trust you'll bear it in mind when you deal with William."

"De Marne and honor are hardly compatible at the moment, Lady Camilla. No doubt he's as unreliable and treacherous as his damned sister."

"I seem to remember you once found Elizabeth amusing and agreeable company."

"That was before—" He broke off.

Camilla looked curiously at him. "Before what?"

"It doesn't matter. Suffice it that in my opinion Lady Elizabeth Oxforth is beyond redemption, as I'm certain her brother will soon prove to be as well."

"How pompous you've become," Camilla murmured.

"And how withered and sour you've become, madam."

"If I'm withered and sour, sir, it's because I have lost the man I loved, the man *you* did nothing to save!"

"Ah, yes, dear Harry. When will you admit that the Harry Summerton who was laid to rest two years ago had changed from the man you insisted upon marrying when you were twenty? The old Harry was everything to be admired, but toward the end I found nothing to admire in him at all. Or do you deny that he had become sharp, selfish, and uncaring?"

"I deny every word!" she cried.

"Madam, the blinkers you wear are entirely appropriate for the mule that you are." He sketched a scornful bow. "Well, I think we've said enough, don't you? I trust you soon mean to remove yourself back to Gloucestershire and that it will be at least two more years before we encounter each other again."

"My sentiments precisely, sirrah, for when I'm faced with you, I find the thought of far-off Gloucestershire very appealing indeed."

"Good. Pray go there as soon as possible." Inclining his head coldly, he turned and left the door, leaving the door open behind him so the sounds and color of the ball swept more loudly over her.

Furious tears stung her eyes, for she felt she'd come off worst in the bitter exchange. She stared after his tall figure, and suddenly she found herself remembering a long past spring afternoon. It was fifteen years ago, just before her marriage. Harry had promised to take her to a boating party on the Serpentine in Hyde Park, but at the last minute he'd been unable to come. He'd sent Dominic instead.

They'd walked together among the daffodils and sailed on the glittering water, and she realized she was drawn to him more than she should be. He'd been different then, charming, witty, and warm, and to be with him was such a pleasure. But there had always been another side of him, a dark and dangerous side of which she was sometimes a little afraid. Perhaps that was what made him so devastatingly attractive. It was certainly what colored her opinion of him now . . .

That day in the park she knew he was drawn to her as well, but neither of them said anything or attempted to take matters further. He'd driven her home afterward, and at the door had raised her hand to his lips. The moment was caught in her memory, jewel-bright and exquisite, like a brilliantly executed miniature, for in those few seconds she knew that if she'd met Dominic before Harry, he would have been the one for her. His touch had blazed through her veins, and his glance kindled a fierce desire that was to burn endlessly over the following years. It excited her to wonder how it would be to kiss him, to lie naked in his arms, to gladly relinquish her virginity to him . . .

She'd been ashamed of these secret thoughts, which made her feel unfaithful to Harry. She was also confused, for how could she love Harry so much, and yet desire his friend? There was no question about the strength of her love for the man she was to marry, but the sense of powerful attraction toward Dominic was with her all the time, especially at nights, when he invaded her sleep. In her dreams she surrendered completely, time and time again . . .

After that she tried never to be alone with him, but it hadn't always been possible. Sometimes they'd been flung together unavoidably, and on those occasions the atmosphere between them had been charged, like the air before a thunderstorm. She could only hope that, unlike Elizabeth, Harry had never become aware of it.

As she stood there, the guilty past faded away, and the glitter of Carlton House swept back. She pulled herself together sharply. This did no good. She'd once found Dominic more attractive than she should, and couldn't forgive herself. Or him. Meeting him again tonight would have been deeply upsetting even without the unfortunate circumstances involving Sophie and William. Now it was impossible to stay on at the ball, or even in London. She'd return to Cavendish Square immediately and tell Hawkins, her butler, that she was going back to Summerton Park as soon as arrangements could be made.

Gathering her skirts, she hurried to the room where all the outdoor garments were kept. Then, clad in her crimson velvet cloak she ordered her carriage and went to wait at the main entrance.

As she waited, Elizabeth approached her again. "You're leaving already, Camilla?"

"Yes."

"But—"

"I've had a very disagreeable skirmish with Dominic, and it's more than I can stand. I can't bear to be anywhere near that man, and London simply isn't big enough. I've decided to go home to Gloucestershire as soon as I can."

"Oh, I'm so sorry, Camilla, but it's probably for the best. Just promise to come back for the wedding."

"The wedding? Oh, William and Alice." Camilla felt dreadful. Should she say something about what had happened tonight? She didn't want to leave Elizabeth in the dark, but if William abided by his word not to see Sophie again there was surely no need for his sister to know anything. Was it perhaps a case of allowing sleeping dogs to lie? Yes, it was, she decided.

Elizabeth looked curiously at her. "What is it? Is something wrong?"

"No, nothing at all." Camilla smiled.

"Dominic must have really upset you."

"He did." Camilla found herself wondering what it was that had colored his opinion of Elizabeth, whose infidelities were legion, but who was surely never guilty of anything else.

At last her carriage drew up, but as a footman lowered the rungs and opened the door, she remembered Elizabeth's husband. "Did you know George is leaving the ball to go to Brooks's? In fact, he's probably already gone."

Elizabeth's eyes brightened. "Oh, good."

Camilla was a little cross. "You really are the limit, Elizabeth Oxforth. George is a good man, and you should value him much more than you do."

"Why should I do that when he clearly prefers the card table to my company?"

"Perhaps he chose the card table because of your incessant *amours*," Camilla pointed out.

"Just like chickens and eggs, Camilla, one will never know which came first. I know I'm unkind to

George, but I just can't help it. He brings out the worst in me."

"You'll lose him one day, Elizabeth, and then you'll appreciate what you've forfeited."

"I'm surprised you defend George when you know he didn't care much for Harry," Elizabeth said then.

"George has always been kind to me, and I have always liked him."

Elizabeth gave her a wicked grin. "If you're so fond of him, you can borrow him for a while if you like."

"Elizabeth!"

"I'm sorry, but I simply couldn't resist it." Elizabeth chuckled and then kissed Camilla's cheek. "Write to me when you get home."

"I will."

"*Au revoir*, Camilla."

"*Au revoir.*"

Elizabeth stepped back as the carriage swept out of Carlton House into Pall Mall.

Chapter 4

Cavendish Square was quiet. A carriage drove past as Camilla alighted, but most of society was at Carlton House. She inhaled the icy night air. It smelled of the city, reminding her how much she missed the fragrance and freshness of the countryside.

The vigilant butler opened the door as she approached. "Welcome back, my lady," he murmured as he assisted her out of her cloak in the warmth of the entrance hall.

"Thank you, Hawkins. Is everything all right?"

"Yes, my lady."

She turned to him. "I've decided to cut short my stay here and return to Summerton Park."

"Very well, my lady."

"Make arrangements for us to leave the day after tomorrow. That's the thirty-first of March," she added, in case he should be confused by the exceedingly late hour at which she was informing him.

"I understand, my lady."

"That will be all."

He bowed and she went slowly up to her room, where her maid was waiting. Her name was Mary Brown, and she was from Summerton, the village after which the park was named. The Browns were one of the oldest families in the neighborhood, and had always served the big house. Mary was twenty years old, a gentle creature with fair hair and hazel eyes who'd been taken on when her predecessor married a Tetbury innkeeper.

Mary didn't care much for London and so was delighted at the prospect of an imminent return to the country. She hummed as she helped her mistress out of her ballgown.

Camilla lay awake in bed. The faint light of dawn was approaching and she hadn't slept at all. Suddenly she heard a frantic knocking at the front door, and she sat up in alarm.

The urgent hammering continued, arousing the whole household. The startled servants emerged from their rooms as Hawkins took a lighted candlestick and went downstairs with a coat on over his nightshirt. As he opened the door, the distraught caller burst tearfully into the hall.

"I must speak with Lady Camilla! *Est-ce qu'elle est ici?* Is she here? Please let me see her!"

It was Sophie! Camilla's lips parted in dismay. Oh, no, please not the czar's ward, who spelled trouble with a capital *T*! Flinging the bedclothes aside, she hurried from the bedroom.

"Mademoiselle? Whatever is it? What's happened?" she cried anxiously as she went down to the hall, where Hawkins's candle provided the only light.

"Oh, Lady Camilla!" Sophie ran tearfully into her arms. "I'm so unhappy, so very, very unhappy!"

Hawkins dithered disconcertedly nearby. He looked a little ridiculous with his wispy gray hair peeping around his nightcap and his bony legs protruding beneath his nightshirt. The candlelight flickered over his face, and shone pinkly through his fingers as he tried to steady the dancing flame. "Is—is there anything I can do, my lady?" he asked.

"Yes, see the drawing room is lighted and then bring some chamomile tea."

"My lady."

Sophie sobbed distractedly, and was still doing so when the second-floor drawing room was ready and she was ushered to a sofa by the fire. Camilla sat down beside her and took her hand. "What is it, mademoiselle? What's wrong?"

But Sophie's tears only increased.

Camilla's anxiety increased. "Mademoiselle, you *must* tell me what's wrong. You should be with Lady Cayne and Lord Ennismount, so what are you doing here?"

Sophie was still too overwrought to respond, and at last Camilla was obliged to shake her a little. "Please stop crying, mademoiselle, for how can I help if you won't say anything to me?"

Sophie struggled to stem the tears. "They—they won't let me see William anymore. Oh, Lady Camilla, *Vous êtes mon ami, oui?*"

"I'm your friend? Well, I—I suppose so, but I hardly know you, mademoiselle."

Sophie clutched her hand. "Oh, you *must* be my friend, mine and William's! I know you did not tell about us, because Lord Ennismount told me how he lay in wait and saw you leave the music room with William." She pressed her lips together defiantly. "I hate Lord Ennismount!"

Evidently Dominic had handled matters with all the

gentleness of a mallet, Camilla thought angrily. "Sophie . . . May I call you Sophie?"

"But of course."

"Sophie, I'm sure Lord Ennismount didn't mean to upset you."

"Oh, yes he did!" Sophie interrupted heatedly. "He wagged his finger at me and told me I was undutiful!"

"Sophie, I know this isn't the time to point this out, but you *are* undutiful. You're to be betrothed to Prince Ludwig, a fact that neither you nor William troubled to tell me."

Sophie got up agitatedly. "I know, and I am sorry. Oh, this is all so terrible, for I hate Prince Ludwig. He is a—a coxcomb!"

"Possibly, but the Grand Duchess Catherine has arranged the match, and the czar is fully in favor."

"He always is when the grand duchess wishes anything," Sophie replied. "They think it is an excellent match politically, but some years ago I met Prince Ludwig in St. Petersburg, and we loathed each other on sight. I will *never* submit to being his wife."

"I fear you have little choice in the matter. As the czar's ward you are—"

"Entirely in his hands. I know."

"Then you also know it's very wrong of you to see William, who is also in the wrong because he's already betrothed to someone else."

"He doesn't love her, he loves me!" Sophie cried passionately.

"Sophie, William's father is determined he is to marry Alice Penshill. If William refuses, at the very least he'll have his allowance stopped."

Sophie's lower lip jutted obstinately. "My fortune is sufficient for us both."

"Your fortune will depend upon the czar's pleasure, as you're well aware, and I doubt if he'll be pleased to learn you've defied his wishes," Camilla pointed out. "As for William's father, I imagine he'll turn blue with rage if he finds out, for he expects to be made a marquess but certainly won't be if his son is at the center of a monumental scandal that is bound to cause bad feeling between Britain and Russia! He'll do far more than just stop William's allowance—he'll throw him out altogether. Is that what you want? William's disinheritance and disgrace? Oh, Sophie, you must see this love affair has to end."

"William is everything to me, and I would do anything for him, except give him up," Sophie declared vehemently.

Camilla was uneasy. Just how far had the matter gone? "Sophie, forgive me for asking this, but have you and William . . . ?" Oh, there was nothing for it but to be blunt. "Sophie, are you and William lovers in every sense of the word?"

Sophie was indignant. "Lady Camilla, William would not do such a thing, for he is a true gentleman and respects me!"

"I trust so." Camilla looked at her. "How did you know where I live?"

"I—I asked William."

"William? You've spoken to him since the music room?"

Sophie fidgeted guiltily. "Yes, but only for a moment or so, truly. It was after Lord Ennismount and Lady Cayne lectured me, and told me William had agreed to leave straightaway for Scotland so he cannot see me anymore."

"Scotland?"

"Sir George Oxforth has an estate there."

"Ah, yes." Camilla lowered her eyes. Dominic said he'd give William a verbal drubbing, and seemed to have done just that. Nor can he have minced his words if the young man was going straight to Scotland!

Sophie blinked back her tears. "I was so upset because I knew I would never see William again, so I ran to find him before he left Carlton House. We said only a few words before Lord Ennismount came after me."

"And during those few words you asked William where I lived?"

"Yes." Sophie looked reluctantly at her. "You see, I have decided to run away, and you are the only friend I have here in London."

"Run away? Oh, on no account are you to do that!"

"I will not stay to see the Grand Duchess Catherine." Sophie's jaw was set rebelliously.

Dire political consequences loomed on the horizon. Oh, the trouble this young woman could cause if she chose. Camilla felt very awkward. "I wish you hadn't involved me like this, Sophie. I'm already in enough trouble because I fibbed for you earlier tonight, and apart from that I feel at fault for not saying anything to William's sister. Lady Elizabeth is a close friend."

"I was sure you would understand." Sophie sniffed unhappily.

"I do understand, Sophie, but my advice is that you return to Carlton House right now. A ball as important as tonight's is bound to still be in progress and your absence may not have been discovered. I can take you back—"

"Oh, please don't return me to Lady Cayne and

Lord Ennismount!" Sophie cried, fresh tears springing to her eyes.

"Be reasonable, Sophie. I can't possibly hide you and say nothing. Besides, you won't be at Ennismount House for long, as soon as the grand duchess arrives you'll go to her."

"That is even worse." Sophie sat down disconsolately on the sofa. "I—I thought that because you told a fib for me earlier on . . ."

"I'd do it again?"

"Yes." Sophie fiddled with a frill on her ballgown.

"Well, I'm sure it seems very simple and straightforward to you, but I see it a little differently. Besides, I can't with any honesty say I acted solely out of concern for you in the music room, and have to confess to an instinctive urge to thwart Lord Ennismount," Camilla admitted.

Sophie smiled then. "I like you more and more, my lady."

"You're a mischievous minx, Sophie Arenburg," Camilla observed dryly, and with masterful understatement.

Sophie became more contrite. "I do not mean to be. Oh, my lady, I do not like the Grand Duchess Catherine, for she is the one who imposed this horrid match on me. I don't want to go to her."

"I don't think you're in any position to refuse," Camilla pointed out practically, wondering what she was expected to do about it.

"They can't make me do what I don't want to do!" Sophie's lower lip jutted again.

Camilla had to look away, for now she'd been in Sophie Arenburg's company a little longer, it was impossible not to see what a handful the girl was. Surely there could be no doubt Sophie was Czar Alexander's illegitimate daughter, for she conducted herself with all the arrogance of a Romanov!

Sophie looked urgently at her. "I cannot bear to go back to Lady Cayne, nor do I wish to go to the grand duchess."

"Sophie, you must be sensible about this," Camilla pointed out a little wearily. This was getting nowhere.

The girl sighed unhappily. "Lady Camilla, you are not so old you do not remember what it is like to be in love. Lord Ennismount knows nothing about the heart, for he does not have one, nor does his horrid aunt. As for the grand duchess . . ." Words failed Sophie, and she sighed again.

"I'm not quite in my dotage yet," Camilla retorted a little huffily. Not so old? She was thirty-five not ninety-five, for heaven's sake!

"Please do not be offended, Lady Camilla," Sophie begged.

Camilla looked at her. "Enough of this chitter-chatter, miss, it's time to get to the point."

"The point?"

"Don't look so wide-eyed, for you know what I mean. Why, exactly, have you come to me?"

"I—I told you . . ."

"You've told me something, but not everything. You have another motive, don't you?" Camilla held her gaze.

Sophie's eyes filled with tears. "I'm so unhappy, Lady Camilla," she whispered. "I do not wish to cause trouble, truly I don't, but I will not be able to help myself if I am made to go to the grand duchess."

"Everyone is capable of preventing themselves

from causing trouble, Sophie," Camilla replied trenchantly.

Sophie scowled for she wasn't used to being repri-
manded, but almost immediately she realized the
scowl didn't assist her case and so resumed her heartbroken imploring. "Please let me stay with you. If—if
you could just send word to Lord Ennismount and
Lady Cayne, telling them I am safe and well . . . ?"

"It's out of the question, for I can't blithely sweep
protocol aside without so much as a by-your-leave.
Others are already responsible for you, Sophie, and
anyway, I'm leaving for Gloucestershire the day after
tomorrow."

"Gloucestershire?" Sophie's eyes brightened per-
ceptibly.

"Yes. I've had more than enough of London."

Sophie was suddenly more determined than ever.
"Please take me with you, Lady Camilla. I will be
very good, truly I will, and if I am in the country with
you, then I cannot make trouble with the grand
duchess. Is that not so?" she added artfully.

Camilla almost admired the girl's audacity. "You
sly minx!"

"*Oui,* I admit it. I know I cannot defy the grand
duchess and the czar, but I also know I can make
things very awkward for the government here. All I
want is time. I know how horrible Prince Ludwig is,
and with luck the grand duchess might soon realize it
too."

"So much for your impulsive decision to rush here
to me. You've actually given this a great deal of
thought, haven't you?"

Sophie gave a rather penitent smile. "Not a very
great deal, Lady Camilla, but you see I grew up in St.

Petersburg, and I learned how to use things to my own advantage. I must barter for my happiness."

"You barter very well," Camilla said dryly.

"Let me go with you to Gloucestershire," Sophie pressed.

"Even if I agreed, and the Prince Regent and the prime minister consent as well, what are the grand duchess and Prince Ludwig going to say?"

"Ludwig? He doesn't matter," Sophie replied dismissively.

"But he *does* matter; he's going to be your husband, Sophie," Camilla persisted.

"He will not wish to meet me any more than I wish to meet him. At St. Petersburg he was only interested in actresses and women of easy virtue."

"Sophie!"

"Well, it's true. Everyone knew it."

"All right, if you don't think the prince is of any importance, you at least have to concede that the grand duchess is a different matter. *She* won't be in the least amused if you aren't in London to meet her."

Sophie wasn't bothered about this either. "She can be told there is influenza where I am staying. She is terrified of illness, and will not wish me to be anywhere near her."

"You seem very sure."

"I am."

Camilla had to smile. "I'm beginning to feel sorry for Prince Ludwig if he has to marry you," she declared. "I'm also beginning to wonder if William stood any chance at all once you'd set your scheming cap at him."

"I did not scheme to love him, Lady Camilla, it just happened," Sophie replied simply.

Camilla got up. Oh, drat the girl, she had a way of turning everything into a tug at one's heartstrings. But whatever her faults, Sophie Arenburg held the trumps at the moment.

Hawkins came in with the chamomile tea, and as he put the tray down Camilla decided to at least let Sophie stay for the rest of the night. "Hawkins, have the principal guest room made ready as quickly as possible, if you please, and tell Mary I wish her to attend Mlle Arenburg while she's here."

"My lady."

Sophie's eyes gleamed triumphantly. "Oh, Lady Camilla . . . !"

Camilla continued to look at the butler. "Then I wish one of the footmen to prepare to go to Carlton House with a message for Lord Ennismount. I haven't yet decided the exact wording of the message, but will do so presently."

"My lady." He bowed and withdrew.

Sophie was victorious. "You *are* my friend, Lady Camilla!"

"Actually, I have the uncomfortable feeling I'm more your gull than you friend." Camilla gave her some of the chamomile tea. "Here, drink this, it will calm you a little, for in spite of your considerable guile you are most definitely overwrought."

Sophie accepted the cup. Cradling it in both hands, she smiled at Camilla. "I'm so happy I can go to Gloucestershire with you."

"Now, wait a moment. All I've agreed is that you can sleep here until Lord Ennismount is informed about your, er, bartering," Camilla warned. "I can't say whether or not you'll get your way."

"But you are agreeable to what I ask?"

"Yes, I'm agreeable, but I can't speak for the prince and everyone else."

"If they refuse I will threaten to make scene after scene with the grand duchess, I will tell her the Prince Regent dislikes her personally, that he opposes many of the czar's plans, that he and the British government have been advising me against marrying Prince Ludwig, that—"

"You've made your point," Camilla interrupted hastily. She wasn't used to dealing with such single-minded, hotheaded, devious young women and it suddenly seemed an unconscionably long time since she'd been Sophie's age herself.

Sophie looked earnestly at her. "I do not want to say any of these things, Lady Camilla, but I must if I am to get my way."

Camilla didn't know what to say to this undeniable logic. "Well, you've finished the tea and I think it's time you went to bed."

Sophie allowed herself to be led from the room, and was soon installed in the guest room, with Mary fussing around her. She and the maid were much of an age, and as Camilla withdrew she heard them begin to chatter together.

Camilla went to her own room and held the curtain aside to look out at the misty dawn. "I have the most awful feeling you've bitten off more than you can chew, Camilla Summerton," she muttered.

Chapter 5

As it happened there was no need for the running footman to go to Carlton House, because Sophie's disappearance had already been discovered and Dominic guessed where she might have gone. He'd overheard some of the snatched conversation with William before the latter left, and knew she'd asked where Camilla lived. When she then vanished, it was simple enough to deduce she'd gone to Cavendish Square, and so he set off in pursuit.

The footman's departure had been delayed because an alarm was raised when a burglar was seen climbing over the wall from the mews lane behind Camilla's house. Heavy mist obscured everything as the intruder dropped down into the garden, and he wouldn't have been detected at all if it hadn't been for a maid returning to the house after spending the night with her family. She screamed and in a moment the whole household was aroused, but the burglar managed to scramble back over the wall and make his getaway in the mist.

The neighborhood houses were alerted by the shouting, and by the time Dominic's town carriage drew up at the door it seemed every servant in the square was out searching. Flaming torches smoked and flickered in the haze, and shouts rang around the houses as he alighted and stood toying with his cuff.

"What's going on?" he demanded of a passing groom.

"Someone tried to break in at Lady Camilla Summerton's, sir," the man replied.

Dominic hurried to Camilla's door, and knocked loudly.

Hawkins peered warily out brandishing a brass candlestick, and Dominic stepped hastily out of range.

"For God's sake take care, Hawkins! It's me!"

Hawkins recognized him from the days when he'd been a frequent and welcome caller. "Lord Ennismount? Oh, forgive me. There was a burglar, and—"

"Is Lady Camilla all right?" Dominic interrupted quickly.

"Oh, yes, my lord."

"Good. Now then, is Mlle Arenburg here?"

"She is indeed, my lord. Her ladyship was about to send word to you. Please come in."

As Dominic entered, Camilla came down the staircase tying a frilled pink woolen wrap over her nightgown, and she halted in dismay to see him standing in the hall. For a moment she didn't know what to say, but then she descended the final steps. "Since my footman has yet to leave for Carlton House, I must wonder why you've called at this address in your search for Mlle Arenburg, my lord."

A light passed through his eyes. "Before you leap to conclusions, Lady Camilla, I didn't come because you are in suspicion, but rather because I overheard Mlle Arenburg asking de Marne for your address."

"I wish you to know I neither aided nor abetted her in this foolishness about running away."

"I have no reason to suspect you did, madam. May I see her?"

"She has retired for the night."

"Nevertheless—"

"She has retired," Camilla said again, facing him squarely. "You may as well know she's issued what I can only describe as an ultimatum."

"A what?"

"An ultimatum, although she prefers to say she's bartering."

"Does she indeed? Well, no doubt she'll inform me in due course, but first I must take her back to—"

"She doesn't want to go," Camilla interrupted. "She wants to stay with me, and accompany me to Summerton Park when I leave the day after tomorrow."

He stared at her. "That's out of the question."

"Which is exactly what I said, but it's what she wants, and if she doesn't get it, she threatens to make as much trouble as she possibly can. Among other things, she threatens to tell the grand duchess the Prince Regent and the government have been actively advising her against the Prussian match, and she's very capable indeed of doing just that."

Suspicion darkened his eyes. "I thought you understood that what I told you earlier was restricted information!"

She drew back angrily. "Do you imagine I've put her up to all this?"

"Let's just say I find it hard to believe the contrary."

"No, sir, let's just say that the young lady is a little more cunning than you've given her credit. She grew up in the St. Petersburg court and learned a trick or two about looking after her own interests!"

"She's a troublesome little baggage who's being accorded far too much importance!" he snapped.

"Possibly, but she has the whip hand right now."

He didn't reply.

Camilla exhaled slowly. "She's in love, sir. What was that line from Herrick you were once so fond of quoting? 'Gather ye rosebuds while ye may?' Well, that's how Sophie feels now, my lord. Her future has been mapped out for her, and she doesn't like what lies ahead. She loathes Prince Ludwig and adores William de Marne, and she knows that unless she puts up a fight now, she'll be lost forever in a match she despises. She's gathering those rosebuds, sir, and if they're proving a little thorny for the establishment, well, hard luck!"

"How very impassioned you are, to be sure," he murmured coolly.

"And how unfeeling you are—to be sure," she retorted.

"Unfeeling? My God, that such a charge should hang on *your* lips, madam!"

"A great many charges hang on my lips where you're concerned, sirrah, not least that you could have saved Harry's life if you wished," she said quietly, her dark eyes very bright and challenging.

He met her gaze without flinching. "I'm heartily sick of your tedious accusations. The trouble with you is your conscience isn't as clear as you'd like it to be."

She was trembling. "I hate you," she whispered.

"The feeling is mutual, madam. Now then, are you going to let me see Mlle Arenburg now, or not?"

"Not until she's awake."

"I'm not leaving until I've spoken to her."

"Then you'll have to wait." She pointed to the double door across the hall. "There is the drawing room, my lord, I'm sure you'll be comfortable on the sofa until Mlle Arenburg is able to receive you. Hawkins?"

The butler had been standing close by throughout their bitter exchange, and gave a slight start as she suddenly addressed him. "My lady?"

"Serve Lord Ennismount any refreshment he requires."

Hawkins bowed.

Her eyes flashed toward Dominic again. "I trust you're kept cooling your heels for a good few hours, sir," she said cordially, and then turned to go back up the staircase again.

He gazed furiously after her, but knew it would be wiser to leave matters at that.

Hawkins waited uncomfortably. "Er, is there anything you require, my lord?" he asked after a moment.

Dominic continued to watch Camilla. "Yes, a poisoned chalice," he muttered.

"Sir?"

"It doesn't matter. Well, actually there is something. The Prince Regent must be informed of the situation, to prevent any alarm on account of Mlle Arenburg's safety. Would you tell my coachman to drive to Carlton House and tell Lady Cayne to inform His Royal Highness the young lady is safe and will remain here for the moment? The coachman may then return to Ennismount House, and I will make my own way back when I'm ready."

"My lord."

Turning, Dominic strode toward the drawing room. If Camilla thought he'd leave rather than endure the discomfort of her sofa, she was very much mistaken. And when willful Sophie Arenburg awoke, she was going to find him waiting, although God knows what he was going to do with her. She had him in a bind, and the Prince Regent and entire British government as well.

He went to the fire, leaning a hand on the mantel and gazing into the glowing coals. Damn Sophie Arenburg, damn William de Marne, damn all creation! His thoughts were savage as his fingers drummed. He hadn't wanted the task of watching over the czar's ward, and he certainly hadn't wanted to cross swords with Camilla again.

Straightening, he thought of times gone by when he'd received a warm welcome in the Summerton household. The fire shifted in the hearth, and he turned instinctively toward the door, remembering an evening in the drawing room of their rented house in Park Lane. It wasn't long after Harry and Camilla were first married, and he'd gone there to accompany them to the theater. Originally there had been a foursome, but the young lady he'd been escorting had cried off at the last moment. Now he couldn't even remember her name. She'd never been important anyway. He'd waited by the fireplace just as he was now, and the coals of that other fire had shifted in the hearth as Camilla came in.

She wore a low-cut satin gown the color of wild roses, and there was a dainty jeweled comb in her dark hair. She was twenty years old, lithe, fresh, and enchanting, and she seemed to light up the room as she came to greet him.

"How dashing you look tonight, Dominic," she

murmured, closing her white-gloved fingers warmly over his.

"And how very beautiful you look, Camilla."

"You have a way with words, sir, for I know I'm not beautiful."

"You are to me." The response slipped naturally from his lips, for it was the truth.

Their eyes met, hers so dark and expressive they always arrested his attention. But what could he read now in that enigmatic gaze? Desire to match his own? He felt her hands tremble a little in his, and his glance moved briefly to the flawless curve of her breasts. His body stirred as desire flooded into his loins. Damn it, he wanted her so much he could have taken her right there. He longed to caress those breasts and draw their firm tips into his mouth, he ached to feel her arch beneath him as he slid into the fastnesses of her soul, and he yearned to hear her call out his name as he took possession. His name, not Harry's . . .

Instead there was polite conversation. Stilted, but polite. She drew her hands slowly away. "I warrant half the women in London would die for your compliments, Dominic."

"Half the women in London wouldn't receive my compliments."

"Then I'm doubly flattered."

"Camilla—"

"Yes?"

"Are you and Harry happy together? I mean, really happy?"

Her eyes fled to meet his again. "Yes, of course."

"You have no regrets?"

She didn't reply immediately. "Lord Ennismount, what manner of question is that to ask a new bride?"

"I think you know."

Her breath caught. "Please, Dominic . . ."

For the briefest of moments he touched her cheek. "Don't be fearful, for I'm not about to say it aloud."

"You must never say it." She moved away from him, keeping her eyes averted for a long moment as she struggled to regain her composure. When she spoke again it was to make a lighthearted remark. "I—I'm very fortunate to be escorted by two gallant gentlemen tonight."

"Two? Who is the other fellow?" he countered in the same manner.

She smiled gratefully. "I do believe I've forgotten his name. Let me see, what was it now? Tom? Dick? No, I have it. Harry."

Then Harry himself appeared in the doorway behind them, his golden hair bright in the light from the chandeliers. "What's this? My wife and my best friend indulging in a flirtation?"

A flush of color stung her cheeks. "Hardly a flirtation," she murmured, going to kiss his cheek.

Harry grinned, slipping his arm around her tiny waist as he glanced toward the cognac decanter on the table. "Have we time for a noggin before we leave?"

Camilla shook her head quickly. "No, let's go now, or we'll be late."

"As you wish."

There had been ample time, as she well knew, she just hadn't wanted to linger because Harry's humorous observation about flirting was a little close to home. The color remained on her cheeks, and she was very quiet during the drive to Drury Lane, but during the performance, when the lamps were subdued and

the audience was enthralled by *Macbeth,* it wasn't at
her husband that she gazed.

Dominic stared into the past, recalling how he'd
felt her eyes upon him. She hadn't looked away when
he turned toward her, and he saw so much written on
her face. All the forbidden, wanton things he knew
were written on his own.

Suddenly the past scattered as Hawkins entered the
drawing room, and it was the present again. "Begging
your pardon, my lord?"

Dominic drew himself up sharply. "Yes?"

"I thought you should know your coachman has left
for Carlton House. He will drive back to Ennismount
House afterward as instructed."

"Thank you."

"My lord." The butler withdrew again.

Dominic took off his coat and flung it unceremoni-
ously over a chair before sitting on the sofa. He
stretched his long legs out and leaned his head back
wearily. He had better things to do than fuss around
after a wayward young woman whose only claim to
importance lay in the identity of her guardian. And
better things to do than sit in this damned drawing
room wishing Sir Harry Summerton had married
someone else all those years ago.

"Gather ye rosebuds while ye may?" He wished to
God that he'd followed Herrick's advice. But it was
too late now. Far too late.

Chapter 6

The mist had become a freezing fog when Camilla rose after only a few hours' sleep. She didn't ring for Mary, but dressed herself in an apricot merino morning gown and tied her long dark hair back with a brown velvet ribbon before sending for Hawkins.

He came immediately. "Good morning, my lady."

"Good morning, Hawkins. Is Lord Ennismount still here?"

"Yes, my lady."

"What a pity. How is Mlle Arenburg?"

"I understand she's well, my lady. She's in her room at the moment."

Camilla nodded. "Tell me, Hawkins, have you commenced preparations for our return to Summerton Park?"

"Yes, my lady. Everything will be ready for tomorrow morning, and I've dispatched a messenger to see the servants there have the house warmed and ready."

"Excellent. There may be a slight change in the plans because Mlle Arenburg might accompany me. It's not settled yet, though. That will be all for the moment."

"My lady."

Camilla went to Sophie's room shortly afterward, but just as she reached it the door opened and Mary came out. The maid seemed startled and almost dismayed to see her. "Oh, my lady!"

"Good morning, Mary. Good morning, Sophie," Camilla replied, entering the room.

Sophie was by the window. She wore a lace-trimmed nightgown Camilla had lent to her, and her blond hair cascaded over her shoulders. She'd been looking down into the square, but turned with a quick smile. "*Bonjour,* Lady Camilla. It is very foggy this morning, *n'est-ce pas?*"

"Yes, it is."

"I cannot see anything outside."

Camilla went to look out as well. The fog swirled silently over the pavement, and the cobbled carriageway vanished into a white gloom. A hackney coach was a mere shadow, and the sound of its passing echoed long after it had ceased to be visible.

Sophie glanced at her. "Winter mornings are misty like this in St. Petersburg, although much, much colder, and always with deep snow and ice."

"I can imagine." Camilla went to hold her hands out to the newly stoked fire.

Sophie watched her. "Lord Ennismount is here, is he not? Mary told me."

"Yes, he came last night, not long after you'd gone to bed."

"You are going to tell me I must go back with him, aren't you?" Sophie's tone was a little accusing.

"No, I'm going to ask you again if you still wish to stay with me."

"Of course."

"Then I will support you when we speak to Lord Ennismount."

"We? I do not wish to speak to him," Sophie replied, the familiar scowl appearing on her face.

"You have to speak to him, Sophie. He's hardly going to take my word for everything you said last night."

"He will try to make me leave with him."

"To try is one thing, to succeed quite another," Camilla observed dryly. Make Sophie Arenburg do something she didn't want to? One might as well try to make a pig fly.

Sophie took comfort from the observation. "That is true. He cannot force me, not when I can make things so awkward."

Camilla eyed her a little crossly. "And you can stop making threats, veiled or otherwise, young lady. I want your solemn promise that you're going to behave yourself while you're with me. You're to conduct yourself decorously, and there certainly isn't to be any contact with William, is that clear?"

"I will not be ordered," Sophie answered, raising her chin grandly and adopting what Camilla was coming to recognize as her St. Petersburg stance. "Czar Alexander is my guardian, and—"

"Oh, spare me," Camilla interrupted wearily. "I like you and want to help if I can, Sophie, but you'll make both feats impossible if you continue in this vein. All these airs and theatricals might be acceptable in St. Petersburg, but this is London, and I'm not prepared to put up with them. Do you understand?"

"Yes," Sophie muttered sullenly.

"I didn't quite hear," Camilla replied, determined to have a more gracious response than that.

"*Oui*, Lady Camilla, I understand," Sophie said politely.

"That's better. Now then, do you want my assistance?"

"Yes."

"Then abide by my rules."

Sophie pouted a little, but nodded. "I will do all you ask, Lady Camilla."

"Do you promise?"

"Yes."

Camilla sighed with relief. "Thank goodness for that. Now then, where has Mary gone?"

"Mary? Oh, I—I asked her to bring me a cup of tea."

She seemed a little uncomfortable, Camilla thought curiously, her puzzlement increasing as she saw an empty cup already on the little table by the pagoda-canopied bed. "More tea? But you've already had some."

"I—I was thirsty."

At that moment Mary returned, but her hands were empty.

Sophie looked crossly at her. "Mary, you have forgotten my tea!"

The maid blinked. "Forgive me, mamselle, I'll get it right away."

Camilla shook her head. "There isn't time now. I want Mlle Arenburg to see Lord Ennismount. Where is the morning gown she selected from my wardrobe last night?"

"Here, my lady." Mary hurried into the adjoining dressing room and returned with an amber marguerite gown.

Camilla turned to Sophie. "Be so good as to get

ready, for the sooner we confront Lord Ennismount, the sooner we'll know if you can remain with me."

As the two young women adjourned to the dressing room, Camilla went back to the window to look out at the square. She wondered how amenable he'd be this morning after spending a few uncomfortable hours on a sofa. But perhaps his disposition wasn't of consequence, for what really mattered was the reaction of the Prince Regent and the government to Sophie's threats. In all probability the girl was going to get her way, for everyone was bound to prefer to see her out of London if she was likely to tell mischievous fibs to the Grand Duchess Catherine.

At last Sophie was ready, and Camilla smiled. "Shall we go down?"

"If we must."

"Oh, we must," Camilla replied firmly, ushering her to the door.

They found Dominic seated by the fire reading the morning newspaper, but he hastily set it aside and rose to his feet as they entered.

Camilla halted before him. "Good morning, Lord Ennismount."

"Lady Camilla." He bowed, and then inclined his head to Sophie. "Mademoiselle Arenburg," he murmured.

"*Milord*," Sophie replied.

Camilla couldn't help thinking anew how handsome he was, and how elegant, even though he'd spent the night in his evening clothes. His dark hair was a little ruffled, and his chin in need of a shave, but somehow he still didn't look less than superb. He was the quintessential aristocrat, cool, poised, and never at a disadvantage. Well, almost never.

He was still looking at Sophie. "What have you to say for yourself this morning, mademoiselle?" he asked.

"That I am sorry I ran away, Lord Ennismount, but I am not sorry I am here with Lady Camilla. I wish to stay with her."

Dominic's blue eyes were coldly penetrating. "Mademoiselle Arenburg, your behavior has been reprehensible in the extreme. Not only have you run away without any thought of the consternation and alarm your disappearance would cause, but you've also been indulging in a clandestine liaison with Lord de Marne. Such a friendship is most definitely out of the question as far as you are concerned, as I think you know full well."

"Are you going to tell tales on me, *milord?*" Sophie's eyes were wide and innocent, but the conclusion to be drawn from her words was only too obvious. *Tell tales on me, and I'll tell some tales of my own!*

Dominic studied her. "No doubt you think you're very clever, mademoiselle."

Sophie took a long breath. "Lord Ennismount, I have made no secret of not wanting to marry Prince Ludwig, but the grand duchess has decided on the match and that is that. But if she has time to see what a beast he is, maybe she will decide against the match after all."

"Beast?" Dominic was a little startled.

Sophie nodded. "Yes, a womanizing beast."

Camilla felt uncomfortable. "Young ladies shouldn't say such things, Sophie."

"But it is the truth. I do not want to be anywhere near him, and that is why I hope I will be allowed to go with you, my lady. The prince will be more interested in the greenroom at Drury Lane than me, and the grand duchess can be told influenza is rife where I am staying. That will make her very glad I'm not with her, I promise you. She has a morbid fear of becoming ill, you see."

"Oh, I see all right, I see you've planned this quite thoroughly."

"I'm doing what I must."

Dominic's eyes swung to Camilla. Unspoken words hung in the air. "*Gather ye rosebuds while ye may . . .*"

Sophie pleaded with him. "I beg that you let me stay with Lady Camilla, *milord.*"

"It's not up to me."

"But you will speak on my behalf?" Sophie pressed. "I will be good, *milord,* like a little mouse. Lady Camilla will not even know I am there."

Dominic knew he had no real choice but to agree to put her proposition to the relevant parties. "Very well, mademoiselle, I'll see what I can do."

"Oh, thank you, *milord!*" Sophie seemed about to fling herself in his arms.

He went on: "But I have no authority to make the decision, it's up to the Prince Regent and the prime minister, and the Russian ambassador must be consulted as well."

Sophie's face fell. "The ambassador?"

"I think so, don't you? You may be a British responsibility at the moment, but soon you'll be a Russian one again, and the ambassador is the czar's official representative. If they are all agreeable, I'm sure you'll be permitted to accompany Lady Camilla. If not, I'm afraid you must adhere to the original plan and come back to Ennismount House with me in readiness to meet the grand duchess."

"If I cannot have my way in this, I will carry out my threat, *milord*. I will be the most believable liar in all the world! I will say such terrible things to the grand duchess that she will leave London in a huff. She will then repeat everything to the czar, and—"

Dominic interrupted acidly. "Mademoiselle Arenburg, I find you most disagreeable when you behave like this. Are all the czar's wards so disgracefully ill-mannered and selfish, or is it your sole prerogative?"

Sophie flushed. "I—I am not ill-mannered and selfish!" she protested.

"Oh, yes, you are, miss," he snapped.

Sophie glared at him, but then lowered her eyes. "I am sorry *milord*."

"So you should be. Now, if you don't mind, I'd like to speak to Lady Camilla alone."

Without another word, Sophie turned to hurry from the room, and as the door closed behind her, Dominic faced Camilla.

"I trust you know what you're doing?" he said.

"I believe so."

"If you don't, now is the time to say it."

Tell him she felt out of her depth? She'd rather wear sackcloth and ashes! "I'm sure Mlle Arenburg and I will manage very well together, Lord Ennismount," she replied coolly.

"Just be on your guard, for it seems to me these particular young lovers have been a little too easy to part."

"What do you mean?"

"Simply that according to Miss Simmonds, Mlle Sophie Arenburg never gives up without a veritable war of wits, and I have to confess to thinking your old headmistress is probably right. Our little mademoiselle would say anything to get what she wants, she doesn't simply gather rosebuds, she snatches the whole bush up by the root! However, since you're so eager to take her under your wing, I can only presume you have the measure of her."

"Yes, I believe so," Camilla replied.

"I understand you're leaving for Summerton Park first thing tomorrow?"

"That is the intention."

He gave a thin smile. "One can only be thankful you didn't leave it until the day after."

"The day after?"

"April the first."

She colored a little. "How droll, to be sure. Isn't it time you went about your business, my lord? You have much to do if Mlle Arenburg's request is to be considered before I leave."

"Request? What a monumental understatement."

"I did warn you."

He sketched her a bow. "So you did," he murmured, and then went to the door. "Good day, my lady."

"Good day, sir."

She went to the window to watch as he went down the steps from the front door. He paused on the pavement for a moment, his tall figure indistinct in the fog. Then he stepped on to the cobbles and was lost from view. But she felt as if he were still in the room with her. As if he touched her . . .

Chapter 7

It was evening when Dominic returned to Cavendish Square. Camilla and Sophie were playing piquet in the drawing room as his carriage drew up at the door. Sophie heard it first and got up from the little card table to hurry to the window. Her straw taffeta gown was another of Camilla's, there being little point in transferring her own wardrobe from Ennismount House until it was definite that she could remain with Camilla.

Holding the heavy fringed velvet curtain aside, she looked out. "It is Lord Ennismount!" she cried.

Camilla got up. "I think it best if you go up to your room," she said.

"Oh, but—"

"Do as I say, Sophie."

To her relief Sophie didn't argue further, but hurried out just as Dominic's cane was heard rapping at the front door.

Camilla positioned herself before the fireplace, patting her hair into place and then nervously smoothing the rich damson velvet skirt of her gown. Her pulse had quickened, but she gave no outward sign as Hawkins announced him.

"Lord Ennismount, my lady."

Dominic entered and accorded her a courteous but cool bow. "Lady Camilla."

"Sir."

"I've just come from Carlton House after speaking to the Prince Regent, the prime minister, and the Russian ambassador."

"And?"

"They're anxious to keep the matter as quiet as possible, which is very fortunate for de Marne, whose father will not be told of his appalling conduct. They are therefore more than willing for the young lady to stay in your custody for the time being, both here in London and then at Summerton Park."

"What you're really saying is they take her threats seriously," Camilla observed dryly.

"Yes, that is indeed what I'm saying. Prince Ludwig isn't deemed to be of consequence in this, indeed Mlle Arenburg's assessment of him would appear to be accurate, but everyone's very anxious to prevent any difficulty with the Grand Duchess Catherine, even the ambassador, who has a positive aversion of her. Mlle Arenburg is again correct when she claims the lady has a dread of illness, so any suggestion of influenza or some such malady would be adequate for our purposes, but if the czar's ward hopes to rid herself of the Prussian match by all this, I fear she's wasting everyone's time, including her own. The grand duchess is absolutely determined to see it proceed, and the small problem of the bride's willingness is neither here nor there."

"That's a matter for the grand duchess's conscience," Camilla replied.

He gave a thin smile. "And conscience is something of which you and I know a great deal, is it not?" he murmured.

She turned away. "I believe you've delivered your message, sir, so please go now."

"I'm afraid I haven't said all that needs to be said regarding Mlle Arenburg."

"Oh?"

"The Prince Regent has imposed a condition upon the granting of her demand."

"What condition?" Camilla asked warily.

Dominic ran his hand through his hair. "There isn't an easy way of saying this. You see, the prince insists that as a matter of protocol I must accompany you; not only that, he insists that I remain with you for the whole of Mlle Arenburg's stay at Summerton Park."

Camilla stared at him, and then shook her head. "No!"

"I advise you to think carefully."

"I don't need to think where you're concerned! Have you at Summerton Park again? Never!"

"Leave personal feeling out of this, madam, for there are other considerations. It has now been implanted in the royal mind that a probable source of embarrassing trouble can be safely removed, and that's all that matters to him. By insisting I accompany you he continues to accord the czar's ward with the appropriate governmental regard, and if you object for any reason, I doubt he'll view it kindly, indeed I fancy he'll take it as a personal affront."

"Are you telling me I have no choice in the matter?" she demanded incredulously.

"You've chosen to involve yourself in all this, madam, and now you're reaping the consequences. You'd be very unwise to change your plans now. The prince is quite capable of making your social position somewhat, er, untenable."

"This is monstrous!"

"Possibly."

She quivered with resentment. "I vowed never to have you at Summerton Park again."

"And I vowed never to go there, believe me, but neither of us has much option. Mlle Arenburg has hoist us both with her damned petard."

Camilla didn't know what to say. She wanted to tell him to go to hell, but in one thing he was only too right; she had indeed chosen to involve herself. She could have refused to help Sophie, but instead had given in to the girl's pressure. There was nothing for it now but to make the best of an odious situation. "Very well, I agree to the prince's condition."

"I have to travel with you."

"Surely not in the same carriage?"

"I fear so. Believe me, the situation is as disagreeable to me as it is to you, but duty dictates."

She looked away again. The petard was being hoist higher and higher!

He spoke again. "Do I have your promise that Mlle Arenburg will not leave this house between now and tomorrow morning?"

"You do," she replied through gritted teeth.

"And do I also have your promise that any attempt to communicate with de Marne will be prevented?"

"Sir, do you honestly imagine I would do otherwise? I'm well aware of the political delicacy of this whole situation, and have already spoken to both Mlle Arenburg and William de Marne. I therefore find your demand for my promise to be more than a little offensive."

"Then I crave your forgiveness," he murmured in a tone that conveyed the very opposite.

"Oh, I'm sure you do."

"I think we understand each other perfectly, Lady Camilla."

"There's no doubt of it."

"Good. Until tomorrow morning then. *Au revoir.*" He inclined his head.

She didn't respond, and without another word he walked from the room. She heard him with Hawkins and then the outer door closed. A moment later his carriage drove away.

Soon Sophie peeped anxiously around the door. "Am I to come with you, Lady Camilla?" she asked.

"Yes, Sophie, you can come, but so unfortunately must Lord Ennismount!"

Dismayed, Sophie came into the room. "Lord Ennismount?"

Camilla nodded. "The Prince Regent insists."

"I—I am so sorry, Lady Camilla."

"So you should be. Not only have I been drawn into your tangle, but I must suffer the presence of a man I despise! And at Summerton Park!"

"I did not mean it to be like this, Lady Camilla." Sophie looked curiously at her. "Why do you hate Lord Ennismount so much?" she asked.

"It's none of your concern, Sophie."

"No, Lady Camilla." Sophie lowered her eyes, but her interest had been aroused. If Camilla wouldn't tell her, she'd ask Mary. Servants always knew everything. She changed the subject. "Shall we play piquet again?"

Camilla glanced at the card table. "I don't feel like it now."

"Then let us play something else," Sophie suggested.

Camilla shook her head. "I'm not in the mood for anything, except perhaps to catch up on the sleep I forfeited last night. I think you should sleep as well, we have a long journey ahead of us tomorrow."

"Yes, Lady Camilla," Sophie replied meekly. She turned away, but then hesitated. "Will we go straight to Summerton Park, or will we stay a night at an inn?"

"I usually stay at the Cross Keys in Wantage. Why?"

"I—I am merely looking forward to the journey. I like inns."

Camilla found this hard to believe. With all her grandiose St. Petersburg ways, it hardly seemed likely that Sophie would appreciate the charms of mere inns!

Sophie went on. "I stayed at one on the way from Bath. It was exciting."

"Then I hope the Cross Keys does not disappoint you. Good night, Sophie."

"Good night, Lady Camilla." Sophie withdrew.

Camilla remained in the drawing room for a few moments more, and then followed, but as she reached the foot of the staircase there was another knock at the door. Hawkins admitted Elizabeth.

Camilla's heart sank, for she knew the unexpected call must be in connection with William. Did Elizabeth blame her for being involved? She went reluctantly to greet her friend. "Good evening, Elizabeth."

"Oh, Camilla, I simply have to talk to you about William."

"Yes, of course. We'll go to the drawing room."

Elizabeth followed her across the hall, but then

halted as she saw a movement at the top of the stairs. It was Sophie. Elizabeth looked angrily at her. "You! This is all your fault!"

Sophie drew back defensively, and Camilla caught Elizabeth's arm. "It takes two, Elizabeth. Come into the drawing room and we'll discuss the matter."

"If it were not for that little madam . . . !"

Camilla glanced up at Sophie. "Go to your room, if you please."

Sophie gave Elizabeth a defiant look before hurrying away, leaving Camilla to lead Elizabeth into the drawing room, where they sat on the sofa.

Elizabeth promptly dissolved into apologetic tears. "Oh, I'm sorry, Camilla . . ."

"It's all right."

Elizabeth took her hand. "I know I shouldn't blame Mlle Arenburg, but this has all come as a dreadful shock. William told me just before he left for Scotland. I had no idea that he and Mlle Arenburg were . . ."

"Your anger is understandable, for I know how much you love him."

Elizabeth's eyes became reproachful. "He told me you helped him at the ball."

"Yes."

"I wish you'd said something to me before you left. I spoke to you as you were waiting for your carriage, the least you could have done was—"

"I know," Camilla interrupted regretfully. "I almost told you, Elizabeth, but then I thought better of it. You'd already said how worried you were about him, and I didn't want to upset you any more. William told me he wouldn't see Sophie again, and I really thought that was the end of it."

Elizabeth looked away. "He must have taken leave of his senses to pay court to a future princess of Prussia."

"You know about that?" Camilla asked, remembering that Dominic had said Sophie's match wasn't widely known.

"George hears so much at Carlton House," Elizabeth explained. "He was there tonight when Dominic and the Russian ambassador spoke to the prince and the prime minister."

"I see."

"George values his friendship with Prinny. And so do I," Elizabeth went on meaningfully. "Camilla, we might forfeit the prince's goodwill if this continues, and then there's Father's marquessate . . . Oh, the disgrace is too awful to contemplate."

"I'm so sorry, Elizabeth."

"I pray Father doesn't find out about all this, because if he does . . ." Elizabeth couldn't finish.

Camilla squeezed her hand. "But it's all to be kept very quiet, and I'm sure William will do the right thing from now on."

Elizabeth gave a short laugh. "I wish I could feel so certain. Most men would be delighted to have a bride like Alice Penshill, but my brother has to set his sights on the unattainable."

"He's in love, Elizabeth."

"Possibly." Elizabeth looked intently at her. "I—I know Dominic is to accompany you and Mlle Arenburg to Summerton Park."

"George told you that as well, I suppose."

"Yes. Look, Camilla, I feel involved in all this. William is my brother and I want to help him if I can."

"Help him?"

"By defending his good name. Oh, I know he's in the wrong for having paid court to the czar's ward, but I don't want him to shoulder all the blame, which he will if things are left as they are. Prinny and everyone else will be keen to deny any responsibility at all for their negligence, and that means finding a scapegoat. It can't be Mlle Arenburg, although God knows she deserves it, so it will be my brother! Camilla, I must protect my family's reputation."

"I do understand, Elizabeth, and you may rest assured that if anything untoward is said I'll speak up on his behalf—"

"Let me come to Summerton Park as well," Elizabeth interrupted. "I'll make myself ill with worry if I have to stay here in town."

Camilla was aghast. "But you hate the country!"

"I need to be there."

"I—I don't think it's a good idea," Camilla replied carefully.

"But—"

"Listen to me, Elizabeth. It's going to be bad enough putting up with Dominic, but it will be far worse if you're crossing swords with him all the time as well."

"I won't, I swear I won't."

"Be reasonable, Elizabeth, you loathe him as much as I do, and you aren't renowned for biting your tongue, as witness your sharp words to Sophie a few minutes ago."

"I'll be a model of reticence. Please, Camilla, it's important to me."

But Camilla had had enough of being pressured into doing something she didn't want to. "Elizabeth, much as I'd like to oblige you, I really do think it's a bad idea."

"But—"

"No, Elizabeth. There is one thing I will do, though."

"Yes?"

"I promise to send for you if there's any need."

Elizabeth wasn't pleased, but gave in. "I suppose I have no choice but to bow to your wishes."

Camilla was relieved. "It's for the best."

"You promise faithfully to send for me immediately?"

"Of course."

"Then that will have to do." Elizabeth looked at her. "I wish you weren't going now all this has happened. Can't you stay in London after all?"

"I don't have any choice now the Prince Regent is involved. He wishes Sophie to accompany me, and says Dominic must come too. That's the end of it."

"Stay wary of Dominic," Elizabeth said quietly, "for he has never told the truth about how Harry died." She got up then. "I'll go now. Take care of yourself, Camilla."

"And you."

The friends embraced, and then Elizabeth left.

Camilla retired to bed and was soon deeply asleep, although she hadn't expected to be able to do so after such an exacting day. But at two o'clock she awoke with a start and lay there wondering what had disturbed her. Everything was quiet, without so much as a carriage passing by. Puzzled, she threw the bedclothes aside and went to the window.

The street lamps shone on a cold, deserted square, where only one or two windows were lit. The fog had

been dispersed by a chill breeze, but it wasn't strong
enough to rattle the windowpanes or moan around the
eaves. She must have heard something else. Alarm
stirred through her as she remembered the burglar.

Pulling on her warm wrap, she opened the bedroom
door and peeped out into the passage, where a solitary
night light shone on a console table. She listened, and
her heart almost stopped as she thought she heard a
door close somewhere downstairs. She pushed her tangled hair back from her face, wondering if she should
raise the alarm. But what if it was only Hawkins or
one of the other servants? She decided to look.

Going as quietly as she could, she tiptoed down the
staircase, listening all the while. It was gloomy in the
hall, which was only illuminated by the faint glow of
the street lamps shining through the fanlight above the
front door. At the bottom she paused, listening for any
small sound. Everything was still, and she thought she
must have imagined hearing the door, but as she turned
to go back up again she heard voices. They were very
low and came from the direction of the kitchens.

She was a little afraid and hesitated to go any farther, but something prompted her to investigate. The
floor was cold beneath her bare feet as she went toward the door to the kitchens, which opened from the
back of the hall. Now she could definitely hear the
murmur of voices, but as she pushed the door open, its
hinges squeaked loudly. The noise echoed along the
red-tiled passage beyond, abruptly silencing the voices
on the other side of the other door at the far end.

Camilla's heart was already beating swiftly, but
now it began to pound. Her mouth was dry as she
called out nervously. "Who—who's there?"

The silence continued, but after a moment the other

door opened and to her relief Mary peeped anxiously toward her. "My lady?"

"Mary! Oh, I'm so glad it's only you!" Camilla hurried along the passage.

Mary opened the door a little more. "It—it's not just me, my lady. Mamselle is here with me.'

Startled, Camilla went into the candlelit kitchens. Sophie was seated at the scrubbed table with a cup of chocolate. Another cup, evidently the maid's, stood opposite her. Camilla looked from one face to the other. "Why are you here?" she asked Sophie.

"I—I couldn't sleep, Lady Camilla. Mary said she would bring me some chocolate, but I preferred to come down here with her. Have I done wrong?"

"No, of course not. I must have heard you pass my door, for something woke me up."

"We tried to be quiet," Sophie said.

"Yes, I'm sure you did, it's just that after the burglar . . ."

Sophie was contrite. "I did not mean to frighten you, Lady Camilla. Please forgive me."

Camilla smiled then. "There's nothing to forgive." She shivered suddenly, for it was unexpectedly cold in the kitchens.

Sophie saw the shiver. "Mary made too much chocolate. Would you like some too?" She indicated the saucepan on the fire.

"Yes, I think I will. I can't think why it's so cold in here, especially when the fire is still so well lit . . ." Camilla sat at the table.

Sophie smiled. "I think it is only that you were frightened, Lady Camilla," she said soothingly.

"Yes, probably."

Mary hastened to bring another cup.

Chapter 8

Two carriages left Cavendish Square for Gloucester-shire the following morning. The first, a navy blue vehicle drawn by four finely matched bays, bore the Ennismount arms on its doors, and conveyed Dominic, Camilla, and Sophie. The second, which belonged to Camilla, carried Hawkins, Mary, Dominic's man, Thomas, and all the luggage. It was the thirty-first of March, the day the Grand Duchess Catherine and Prince Ludwig were due to come ashore at Sheerness.

The weather was cold, overcast, and blustery, with low clouds scudding across the skies, and there was a dampness in the air that told of heavy rain to come. The coachmen huddled on their seats, their caped coats flapping as they tooled their vehicles one behind the other. A grayness seemed to have settled over the capital, making it look dismal and uninteresting. Smoke was torn from chimneys and dull windows faced the turnpike as the carriages drove swiftly westward. A long day stretched before them, and it would be dark when they reached the Cross Keys in Wantage.

Sophie's wardrobe had been brought from Ennis-mount House, and she'd chosen to wear peacock velvet for the journey. Her blond hair tumbled in dainty ringlets from beneath a plumed hat, and her hands were plunged deep into a warm gray muff. She looked every inch a demure seventeen-year-old miss, with no sign so far today of the St. Petersburg hauteur of which she was so easily capable.

Camilla wore cherry wool, and the color suited her. An elegant little black hat was set jauntily on her head, but it wasn't long before she wished she'd elected to wear something wide-brimmed instead, because Dominic sat directly opposite her and to avoid his glance she either had to give herself a stiff neck by gazing steadfastly out of the window all the time, or a headache by keeping her eyes constantly lowered. A wide brim would have been a very convenient barrier.

She gave him a surreptitious look. How effortless it was for him to achieve that elusive mixture of nonchalance and sartorial perfection that was sought after by every gentleman of the *ton*. Most would have to spend hours before the mirror with their valets, but nature had favored the Earl of Ennismount with a natural gift. He must be the dream of every Bond Street tailor, for he would surely look good in anything! She wished she could fault his appearance today, but how could one criticize the immaculate? He was a man of distinction, from the gleaming spurs on his Hessian boots to the superb frogging on his Polish greatcoat, and she despised every inch of him!

As the minutes passed, she reflected rather sourly that if she could turn the clock back, she'd never have gone anywhere near Carlton House on the night of the ball. Perhaps she'd go even farther back to change matters, and not have left Summerton Park in the first place! Anything, rather than endure what she was enduring now.

Sophie was restless by the time they reached Houn-slow, and positively fidgety when the next stage ended at Slough. She was chattering constantly by the time they changed horses at Henley, and the sound of her voice was beginning to ring in Camilla's ears when the last change of the day took place in late af-ternoon at Wallingford. They set off on the final fif-teen miles to the Cross Keys in Wantage, but were still ten miles short of their destination when the rain that had threatened all day at last began to fall.

It didn't just fall, it poured, drumming on the car-riage roof and swiftly turning the highway into a mire. Progress slowed to a snail's pace as the horses found it more and more difficult to pick their way along the flooded ruts. The first lamps were lit in roadside cot-tages, and the warmth and comfort of the Cross Keys seemed farther away than ever when Dominic sud-denly lowered the window glass and leaned out.

The noise of the rain rushed into the carriage, as did the icy wind that still blustered over the open country-side. He took a moment to gain his bearings, but at last recognized the scenery. "I know where we are. There's an inn ahead, I think we'll break the journey there instead of going on to Wantage," he shouted up to the coachman.

"My lord." The man turned and touched his drip-ping hat.

Dominic drew back into the carriage and raised the window again, before sitting down and brushing the rain from his coat.

Sophie was dismayed. "We are not going to the Cross Keys, *milord?*"

"There's no point in pressing on in weather like

this, especially when the Royal Oak is a creditable enough hostelry," he replied.

"Oh, but we must go on," she declared.

An irritable note entered Dominic's voice. "Mademoiselle Arenburg, if this rain continues the roads will soon be impassable, and I see no point in taking the risk of becoming stranded." He looked at Camilla. "Is the change of plan acceptable to you?"

Sophie turned anxiously to her. "Please let us continue to the Cross Keys, Lady Camilla," she pleaded.

"Sophie, Lord Ennismount is correct to fear we might become stranded. Pressing on would be foolish, especially when there's no need. Besides, we're here now." Camilla glanced out as the carriage drove into the yard of the Royal Oak.

Tears filled Sophie's eyes. "I do not wish to stay here," she whispered.

The carriage jolted to a standstill, but Dominic didn't alight; instead he looked sharply at Sophie. "Why is it so important to go on to Wantage?" he asked suddenly.

She didn't meet his gaze. "It—it isn't important, *milord*," she replied.

"Are you quite sure?"

"Yes."

"I trust so," he said, looking at her for a long moment before flinging the door open and alighting.

Sophie said nothing more as he helped her down into the rainswept courtyard, then she gathered her skirts to hurry to a doorway, where Camilla and Dominic soon joined her. They entered the inn just as the second carriage drove into the yard.

The hostelry was very crowded because of the weather, but as the landlord hastened to secure the last available room for such illustrious guests, Sophie again revealed her anxiety to go on to Wantage.

She looked intently at Dominic. "Please may we stay at the Cross Keys, Lord Ennismount?"

"We've been through all that, mademoiselle."

"But I do not like it here."

"It may not be the Winter Palace, but it will do," he replied in a tone that precluded further argument.

Sophie scowled as he turned away to speak to the landlord, who returned to say that although there was a room for the ladies, Dominic himself would have to sleep as best he could on a settle in the taproom. The food at the inn was of the very highest quality, although the crush in the dining room didn't allow anyone to enjoy it properly. Camilla and Dominic availed themselves of the excellent roast capon, but Sophie pushed her plate away in sulky silence.

If Dominic noticed her sullen mood, he gave no sign, indeed his mind was quite clearly on other things, in particular the pert serving girl who waited upon them. Russet-haired and freckled, she had saucy eyes and a figure that seemed in imminent danger of bursting her low-cut bodice. She was also very forward, and made it clear she was available should Dominic wish.

After a while the way the girl kept deliberately leaning across the table with plates began to irritate Camilla, who wasn't in the least impressed by the ample display of bosom. By the time the gooseberry pie was brought, she'd had enough. "Can you please keep your chest out of my food?" she demanded.

The girl straightened with an offended pout. "I'm sorry, I'm sure," she muttered, walking away.

Dominic smiled appreciatively at the seductive sway of her hips, and Camilla gave him a cold look.

"I had no idea you were so attracted to the obvious and freely available, my lord," she observed cuttingly.

"I would have thought it beneath you to make any comment, my lady," he replied, and she fell into a furious silence, wishing she hadn't made herself such an obvious target.

When the meal was over, Sophie immediately announced she was going to bed, and before anything could be said got up from the table and left the dining room.

Dominic looked urgently at Camilla. "Go with her, my lady, for I don't trust that little minx farther than I can throw her. She's up to something, and we have to be one step ahead of her."

"Up to something?"

"Oh, come now. Don't you think she was extraordinarily anxious to go on to Wantage?"

"Well, yes, but—"

"Think, madam. If she knew that was where we intended to halt, might she not have arranged a tryst there?"

Camilla stared at him. "A—a tryst? But William is in Scotland!"

"So we've been led to believe, but do either of us know for certain that's where he is?"

"Elizabeth said—"

"With all due respect, Elizabeth Oxforth won't know any more than we do. Suffice it that I'm very suspicious indeed of our little Russian miss, and think you should keep a close watch on her tonight."

"I hardly think she's about to . . ." Camilla's voice died away as she noticed the serving girl watching Dominic from a nearby doorway. "So you're concerned about what Sophie is up to, are you, sir? Why aren't you honest enough to simply say you have other things to attend to and merely wish to be rid of me?"

"You're always so free with your accusations, aren't you?"

"With every justification."

"That isn't so."

"I beg to differ. However, one thing is indisputable right now, and that is your disgracefully obvious intentions."

"I'm surprised you care about my nocturnal arrangements, Lady Camilla." He glanced at the serving girl. "She *is* rather sumptuously upholstered, isn't she?" he observed.

Camilla's breath caught. "Do you have to be so—so—?"

"Indelicate?" he supplied obligingly.

"Yes!"

"You are the one who has introduced indelicacy into the conversation, my lady. If my memory serves me correctly, I believe *you* were the one who drew everyone's attention to—"

"And *you* are the gentleman here, so it was up to you to put a swift stop to the 'come hither' conduct of that—that *whore!*" Camilla cried, raising her voice so much that for a moment the entire dining room fell silent. Mortified color flooded into her cheeks, and she lowered her gaze to his wineglass, wishing she wasn't so easily goaded by him.

Dominic's eyes were bright. "I'm of a mind to be flattered that the situation incenses you so much," he murmured.

"I couldn't care less where you spend the night, or who with, Lord Ennismount."

"Then why do you persist in talking about it?" he snapped back.

Somehow she resisted the urge to pick up his glass of wine and throw it over him. Slowly she rose to her feet. "You are contemptible, sir," she said levelly.

He met her eyes. "You're entitled to your opinion, madam, but we seem to have wandered away from the subject of Mlle Arenburg. It doesn't matter how I intend to spend tonight, but it does matter that the czar's ward might still be in touch with de Marne, and since I cannot be at her side every minute until dawn, I fear that duty falls to you. You volunteered to don the cloak of chaperone, so I suggest you tie said cloak tightly around your throat and get on with it!"

Gathering her skirts, Camilla swept from the room, not bothering to accord him a parting word or even a nod of the head. She tossed a cold glance at the serving girl, who pulled an insolent face in return.

Camilla was still angry when she reached the bedroom, but Dominic and the serving girl went from her mind because of the odd way Sophie and Mary's conversation fell away the moment she entered. Sophie was seated before the dressing table while Mary attended to her hair, and they glanced at each other before the maid continued unpinning and brushing.

"Is something wrong?" Camilla looked suspiciously from one to the other.

"No, my lady," Mary replied swiftly, but her manner could only be described as uncomfortable, as if she'd been caught doing something she shouldn't.

Sophie, on the other hand, seemed all that was natural and at ease. "We were just discussing coiffures, Lady Camilla," she said.

Camilla went to the window and held the curtain

aside to look out. Rain ran down the pane, catching the lantern light in the yard. But she could see something else in the glass, the reflection of the room behind her, and so clearly saw the second meaningful glance Sophie exchanged with the maid. So they'd been talking about coiffures, had they? Dominic's warning rang in her ears.

Something had to be said. She turned suddenly. "That will be all, Mary."

The maid hastily replaced the pins and hairbrush on the dressing table and then bobbed a curtsey. "Good night, my lady. Mamselle."

Sophie nodded. "Good night, Mary."

The door closed and Camilla went to the dressing table. "Now then, miss, I wish to have a word with you."

"A word?"

Camilla decided to see how Sophie would react if suddenly confronted with a blunt question. "Did you make arrangements to meet William at the Cross Keys?" she asked.

Sophie didn't flinch. "No, of course not!"

"Do you swear it?"

"It is the truth!" Sophie cried, getting up to face her.

"Is it?"

"Yes!" Sophie's tone was vehement.

"Because if it isn't, you may as well know that I am as capable of blackmail as you."

Sophie was aghast. "Blackmail?" she repeated.

"Yes, for that is what your so-called bartering amounts to. Very well, miss, as you sow, so you reap. You may think that being the czar's ward, with such an important match in the offing, et cetera, et cetera, you are safe from anything I might do, and maybe you're right, but William certainly doesn't enjoy the same immunity, so let me warn you that if you misbehave in any way, I'll see to it that his father learns of his misconduct. You're perfectly aware of the inevitable unfortunate consequences for William's future."

"You—you are *threatening* me?" Sophie cried, with more than a hint of lofty St. Petersburg outrage.

"No, Sophie, I'm bartering," Camilla replied coolly.

Sophie flushed, and for a moment seemed outraged again, but instead she lowered her eyes obediently. "I am being good, Lady Camilla, I swear it. I have not made any secret arrangements."

"I hope I can believe you."

"You can, and you do not need to be so horrible to me."

"It wouldn't be necessary if you inspired a little more faith."

"I can't help it if you do not trust me, Lady Camilla, nor can I help it if you are jealous of an inn serving girl!" Sophie cried resentfully.

Camilla stared at her. "I—I beg your pardon?"

Sophie bit her lip and lowered her eyes quickly. "I did not mean to say that. Please forgive me."

"You meant every word."

Sophie became rebellious again. "Yes, I did! Mary told me what you say about Lord Ennismount, but I can see the truth. You find him attractive, and wish he was to spend tonight with you instead of a low maidservant!"

"That's quite enough, Sophie," Camilla said in a low, trembling voice.

But Sophie couldn't stop now. "You are bitter with him, and you take it out on me!"

"I said that's enough!" Camilla snapped. "Now listen to me, young lady, if you are to stay at Summerton Park as my guest, I expect a certain standard of conduct, especially when it comes to your pronouncements about my private affairs, which have absolutely nothing to do with you. I find it totally abhorrent that you should resort to pumping my maid on such a matter, and even more abhorrent that you should leap to conclusions you're actually prepared to voice. You're proud enough to boast of being the czar's ward, so perhaps it would be a little more becoming if you behaved with more appropriate dignity and decorum."

The rebuke winged home, and Sophie stared for a moment. "I—I am sorry, Lady Camilla," she said in a chastened tone.

"So you should be."

"I—I am very tired. I think I will go to sleep now." Sophie quickly finished her toilet and then climbed into the bed.

It was still raining shortly afterward when Camilla joined her and extinguished the candle, plunging the room into darkness. The rain lashed against the window and sluiced down a drainpipe. There wasn't anyone on the road now, and the yard was quiet. Camilla stared up into the darkness. This had been an exceedingly disagreeable day, and she could only pray tomorrow would be an improvement.

The minutes passed and she began to feel a pang of remorse for having spoken so very harshly to Sophie, even though the girl had richly deserved it. But the czar's ward had touched upon the rawest of nerves. What should it matter if Lord Ennismount spent the night in a tavern wench's arms? What should it matter if he sampled the charms of every maid at the inn?

What indeed. The answer was obvious. It mattered because Sophie was right, Lady Camilla Summerton *was* jealous!

It was a bitter pill to swallow. Camilla stared angrily into the darkness. Oh, curse him! She prayed the serving girl's bed had bugs so he'd be severely bitten for his sins!

But she couldn't hide the truth from her innermost self, for no amount of cursing could prevent the erotic dreams that permeated her sleep that night. In her fantasies she was the serving girl, lying naked between rough sheets as the Earl of Ennismount made fierce love to her. She was at his mercy, his to do with as he pleased, and she cried out her intense enjoyment each time he plunged into her. His need was urgent and compelling, and gratification was all that mattered. He was ruled by his sexuality, driven to thrust deeper and deeper until his desire was released with a convulsive force that shuddered through his entire body.

The sensuous delights that came to her then were more exquisite than any she'd known before, and the pleasure so acute and unbridled that she dug her fingernails into his back as she clung to him. Soon she wanted more and began to caress him again. She was insatiable, and his potency was her equal.

How many times he took her in her dreams that night she didn't know, but she did know that come the morning of All Fools' Day, she wasn't the one he was lying with. All Fools' Day. How appropriate for the singular fool who'd submitted so shamelessly in her sleep. Well, that was where her secret desires would stay—in her sleep! She resolved to ignore him, and take no notice at all of that immoral little flibbertigibbet of a serving girl.

Chapter 9

But like all resolutions, it was one thing to make them, quite another to carry them out. Breakfast was awkward. Sophie picked at her meal again and continued to sulk because they hadn't stayed at the Cross Keys. Dominic, on the other hand, was in what for him was an amiable mood, leaving Camilla to conclude that he had in fact spent a very satisfying night doing all the things *she'd* merely dreamed about!

The impertinent serving girl was very much in evidence, and was the life and soul of Fools' Day. She didn't miss a single opportunity for raucously tricking her fellow servants, whether it was to tell another maid her shoe was unbuckled when it wasn't, or to send one of the waiters for a bowl of water that wasn't required. Camilla began to find the constant squeals of "April fool!" a little too much, especially since between joke playing the girl continued to make eyes at Dominic.

After enduring it all for as long as she could, Camilla could at last stand no more. She waited until the girl leaned over the table again with a pewter coffeepot, and then gave a horrified gasp. "Oh! How awful for you!"

The girl turned swiftly. "What is it?"

"There's an absolutely huge spider in your hair! Ugh, it's gone down the back of your neck!"

The girl gave a scream and dropped the coffeepot as she fled from the dining room, unlacing her bodice as she went. They could still hear her screams long after she'd vanished into the kitchens.

Camilla smiled sweetly. "April fool," she murmured.

Dominic raised an eyebrow. "Tush, madam, that was most unkind."

"I don't know what you mean, sir."

"No, of course not, but as it happens she isn't the only April fool around here."

"Meaning what, precisely?"

For a moment he considered explaining, but then thought better of it. "Oh, it's of no consequence. Please forget I spoke."

Nothing more was said, and soon afterward they left the dining room.

The rain had dwindled away overnight, but it was midday before the road was considered dry enough for travel. Sound carried clearly in air that seemed cleansed by the long downpour, and now the weather was almost bracingly fresh. Most of those who'd stayed at the inn were leaving at the same time, and there was a crush of people and vehicles in the enclosed space. Horses stamped and shook their harness, wheels scraped on cobbles, and grooms shouted.

Dominic handed Camilla and Sophie into the carriage and then went to speak to his coachman, who leaned down in order to listen intently and touched his hat. Then Dominic climbed into the carriage and a moment later it drove out on to the road, followed by the second vehicle containing the servants.

The horses had to pick their way along the ruts, and the travelers soon found the swaying and jolting of the carriage exceedingly wearing. Sophie remained subdued, saying nothing spontaneously and only replying to questions in monosyllables. But even these brief utterances died away into nothing at all as the rooftops of Wantage appeared ahead and the coachman suddenly reined in. He came to the door and Dominic lowered the glass.

"What is it, Harper?"

"I'm sorry, sir, but I fear one of the horses is about to shed a shoe. I think it best if we stop at the Cross Keys to let their smithy take a look."

"Very well."

Sophie sat forward urgently. "We're stopping at the Cross Keys?"

Dominic nodded as the carriage drove on. "Yes, mademoiselle, it seems we are, so your prayers are answered after all."

"Oh, but I don't want to stop there now. Can't we go on?"

He searched her face. "We can hardly continue with a lame horse, mademoiselle, so we'll definitely be stopping at the Cross Keys."

"Oh." She sat back again.

He continued to study her. "How very unpredictable you are, Mademoiselle Arenburg. Yesterday you wanted above all to go to the Cross Keys, now it seems you've changed completely."

She didn't reply, and the carriages drove on into the town. As they drew up outside the Cross Keys, Harper climbed down again and hurried into the yard. Several minutes passed without his return, and at last Sophie sighed dramatically.

"Oh, where is he? Why does he not come back?"

"Have patience, mademoiselle. These things take time," Dominic murmured.

Harper reappeared, accompanied by a burly smith carrying some implements in his grimy hands. Dominic flung the carriage door opened and climbed out to join the two men by the lead horses. Sophie gazed up at the inn's windows, and her tongue passed almost nervously over her lips.

Camilla looked curiously at her. "What is it, Sophie?"

"Nothing."

"You seem ill at ease."

"I merely wish this journey was at an end, that is all."

Camilla leaned her head back, hoping the entire stay at Summerton Park wasn't going to proceed in the same vein as the journey. If it did, the coming days were going to be an appalling endurance test for all concerned. She could hear the murmur of voices as Dominic and the two men spoke together, and then there was the brief sound of a horseshoe being hammered. A moment later Dominic returned to his seat, and the carriage pulled away once more.

After a few minutes, Sophie ventured to speak to Dominic. "Is all well now, Lord Ennismount?"

"Oh, yes, mademoiselle."

She smiled. "Will we reach Summerton Park today?"

"Yes, just before dark," he replied.

Soon Wantage slipped away behind, and as the road dried out more and more, so the horses' pace picked up. The light was just beginning to fade as at last the carriages drove through the village of Summerton and then swept through the lion-topped stone gateposts by the north lodge of the park. Beech trees overhung the drive as it curved down through grounds that were bright with daffodils. The land sloped away toward the river valley where the house was hidden from view.

The setting sun made a final bid for glory, blazing from beneath the final clouds to bathe the landscape in crimson and gold. Birdsong echoed all around, and the windows of the house flashed like fires as the carriages halted by the magnificent Corinthian portico. The birdsong became louder as Dominic flung the carriage door open and alighted. Twilight encroached as the sun sank inexorably toward the western horizon, and Sophie shivered as she accepted Dominic's hand to climb down. There was a raw chill in the air, but the light breeze brought the fresh scent of daffodils and spring blossoms, a pleasant change after the smoke of London. Someone fired a shotgun in the distance and the birds fell silent for a moment. During that brief silence the breeze carried a new sound, soft musical notes that seemed not to follow a tune.

Sophie glanced across the park. "What is that?" she asked.

"Wind chimes," Camilla replied, avoiding Dominic's eyes.

"But where are they?"

Camilla was reluctant to explain but could feel Dominic's coolly mocking gaze upon her, and so she looked directly at him as she answered Sophie. "They're on the pagoda in the Chinese garden."

Sophie's eyes brightened. "There is a pagoda? Oh, I must see it!"

"It's too late now, but you can see it whenever you wish during the daylight." Camilla still met Dominic's eyes. She hated mentioning the pagoda because it held very sensitive, and, for her, embarrassing memories. He shared those memories, but how he felt about them was a mystery. No doubt his calculated amusement now was an indication . . .

Their arrival had been observed and as several footmen emerged from the house, Hawkins alighted from the second carriage to take command. He issued brief instructions as he disappeared into the entrance hall to see if the orders he'd sent ahead had been carried out to the last letter.

Sophie shivered again. "It is cold, *n'est-ce pas?*"

"Yes, it is," Camilla agreed, turning to Dominic. "Shall we go in, sir?"

Elizabeth had described Summerton Park as an opulent oriental temple, and so it was. The whole house might have been plucked from Peking, and the same theme was continued in the grounds, with the pagoda and Chinese garden of which Sophie had just learned. It was all the work of Camilla's late father-in-law, and the entrance hall was the first hint of how greatly he admired chinoiserie of every description.

The pink-tiled floor was laid in a writhing pattern of black dragons and green-and-gold lotus blossoms, and the gleaming white walls were hand-painted with bamboo thickets where fantastic birds showed off their colorful plumage. Immense gilded lanterns were suspended from a celestial ceiling, and there were more heavenly symbols on the heavily carved fireplace, where flames crackled around a fresh log.

Camilla turned toward Hawkins. "Is the drawing room lighted?" she asked.

"Yes, my lady."

"Good. I wish tea to be served there before we go to our apartments."

"My lady." He bowed and hurried away.

Sophie was looking around in delight. "Oh, *c'est incroyable!*" she cried, her eyes shining with approval.

"I'm glad you like it, Sophie," Camilla replied, teasing off her gloves.

"Oh, yes, I like it very much indeed. *J'aime beaucoup la chinoiserie.*"

"Which is as well, given that the entire house is furnished like this." Camilla looked at Dominic, very conscious that this was the first time he'd returned here since Harry's death.

He removed his top hat, and ran his hand through his hair as he glanced around the hall, but then felt her eyes upon him. "It hasn't changed at all, Lady Camilla," he said.

"Oh, yes it has, sir, it's changed in every way now Harry isn't here," she replied, moving toward the staircase to conduct them to the drawing room on the next floor.

He remained where he was. "May I impose on your time for a moment, Lady Camilla?"

She turned. "My time?"

"There was a volume about falconry in your library here. I wonder if I might read it while I'm here?"

She was nonplussed. What an odd moment to choose for an equally odd request. "I—I had no idea you were interested in falconry, sir."

"I daresay you don't know everything about me," he murmured.

"I daresay I don't, sir. Yes, of course you may read the book."

"Perhaps we could get it now?" He held her gaze.

"We? Sir, I know it's two years since you were last here, but I'm sure you remember where the library is." She indicated the doorway opposite.

"I don't quite remember what the book looks like." It was the most lame excuse she'd ever heard him give. What on earth did he want?

"I hardly think I'm any more likely to remember such a book, sir," she said.

A frown darkened his eyes, but he kept his voice light. "Nevertheless, I'm sure two will find it more quickly," he insisted.

She decided to oblige him. "As you wish, my lord," she murmured, turning to walk toward the library, which led off the hall.

Sophie began to follow, but he quickly stopped her. "There's no need for you to be inconvenienced, mademoiselle." He beckoned to a footman. "Please conduct Mlle Arenburg to the drawing room."

Camilla was a little annoyed, for he behaved as if he were the master here!

As Sophie followed the footman, Dominic took Camilla's hand and drew it over his arm to walk toward the library door. "I have something important I wish to say to you," he explained in a low tone.

"That much is obvious, sir," she replied.

"If it was obvious, madam, why did you remain so boneheaded for so long?" he murmured.

She gritted her teeth and declined to respond as they entered the library.

Chapter 10

The library was an oblong pink-and-gilt chamber, warmed at either end by white marble fireplaces with mantels supported by statues of Chinese warlords. The tall bookcases were adorned with gilded trelliswork, and the specially woven rose-pink Axminster carpet bore a golden design of the Chinese god of thunder. There were ornate dragon pelmets above the tall windows, where heavy pink velvet curtains were tightly drawn against the chill of the night.

She searched quickly along the bookcases and soon found the book he'd referred to. "I suppose we must keep up the pretense," she murmured as she gave it to him. "Well? What is it you wish to say?"

"I've been waiting for an opportunity to speak to you alone, but there hasn't been one, so I trust you'll forgive the rather clumsy pretext. The fact is I have every reason to think de Marne is somewhere near here, and that he and Mlle Arenburg are in touch."

Camilla stared at him. "William? Here? But——"

"Hear me out. I've been observing your maid, and believe she's very much in Mlle Arenburg's confidence, probably to the extent of aiding and abetting her by carrying messages."

"Mary? Oh, but—" Camilla broke off and thought for a moment. She remembered conspiratorial voices and the exchange of meaningful glances. "You may be right," she said then.

"You've evidently noticed something."

She explained. "But that's all, I couldn't say I've caught them in anything openly suspicious," she finished.

"No, Sophie Arenburg is too artful for that," he replied, and then went on. "As you know, I concluded yesterday that a tryst had been arranged at the Cross Keys, and today I obtained confirmation."

"Confirmation? How?"

"There was no reason to halt there this morning, my lady, it was simply a ploy. Harper was primed to say he'd found something wrong with the horseshoe, and he took so long to find the smithy because he had something else to do first. I instructed him to inquire of the innkeeper if anyone answering de Marne's description had been there. Well, such a person had not only been there, but had been asking after us. Not only that, he left about an hour before we arrived, and rode west, which suggests to me he was bound for somewhere near here."

Her heart sank. Oh, William!

"I think we may be fairly certain your maid will be involved in any contact Mlle Arenburg has with him."

Camilla didn't know what to say. All she could think of was Sophie's righteous indignation when it was suggested she and William might have arranged a tryst at the Cross Keys. How wide-eyed and innocent the girl had been as she denied everything!

Dominic spoke again. "I don't need to tell you how concerned I am by these developments. It's imperative that Mlle Arenburg is kept away from de Marne, but it won't be easy to achieve if he's hiding somewhere nearby. Short of locking her up . . ."

"We can't do that!"

"More's the pity. God damn de Marne for the shiftless sprig of nobility that he is!"

"William isn't shiftless."

"No? I beg to differ. As far as I'm concerned his entire family is beyond redemption."

"You seem to be somewhat prejudiced, sir."

"With good reason."

She looked quizzically at him. "I trust you mean to explain that remark?"

"No, madam, I don't." He drew a long breath. "Let's get back to the point. We have to collar de Marne, but confronting Mlle Arenburg won't get us anywhere because she's too crafty. I fear we have to be equally as crafty, and the obvious thing is to coerce the maid, but I'm loath to do that just yet for fear of alerting our exasperating young lovers that we're on to them. I want to catch de Marne, not have him slip away unscathed. It's best if we keep the closest eye possible upon their every movement, and act when the right moment comes."

"What do you want to do?"

"You and I will keep Mlle Arenburg under surveillance, and since it now seems clear the maid is in league with our difficult charge, I'll instruct my man Thomas to follow if she leaves the house."

Camilla's lips parted. "Before we left the inn this morning, Mary asked if she could have a little time off to visit her family in the village this evening."

"Then I'd hazard a guess she'll be Mlle Arenburg's messenger as well. They probably know de Marne's whereabouts, or certainly where to leave a note for him to find." He thought for a moment. "I know there are several inns in the neighborhood, but I feel they're all a little too inconvenient for de Marne's purpose. He wants to be close to his sweetheart, not miles away. I've been trying to think of somewhere actually on the estate where he might hide. All that springs to mind is the pagoda."

The pagoda was the last thing she wished to speak about, but she had to reply. "I—I doubt it. It's kept locked now because the stairs inside have become unsafe. Besides, it's visible from the house."

"The outside is, but the inside is an excellent place of concealment, is it not?" he said softly.

Color rushed into her cheeks. "If you're seeking to remind me of—"

"There's clearly no need to remind you, Lady Camilla, you obviously remember full well without prompting."

"It ill becomes you to resurrect a brief lapse on my part."

"A brief lapse maybe, but at the time it was a very telling one," he observed coolly.

Yes, at the time, it was. She was conscious of sliding from the present of 1814 into the past of 1812. The library candlelight brightened into dazzling June sunshine, and suddenly it was the day she'd almost forsaken her marriage vows; the day immediately prior to widowhood . . .

She'd never know if things would have gone the way they had if Harry hadn't been in such an unsociable mood for well over a month. He'd changed before they left London, becoming difficult to please and too easily disposed to criticize her for little or nothing.

He'd even taken to sleeping in another bedroom, although he explained the latter by saying he was very restless and didn't want to disturb her. She was hurt and bewildered, but when she tried to ask him about it, his response was always brusque.

Dominic was with them for the stay, and the contrast between Harry and him could not have been greater. Harry's presence was oppressive; Dominic provided devastatingly tempting distraction. Something seemed to have emboldened him, for he began to make it more subtly clear he found her desirable. When he smiled at her, she became the only woman in the world, and it was a heady feeling. Undercurrents began to swirl between them, building up into a flood tide that almost overwhelmed them one glorious June afternoon.

They'd all three gone for a picnic, although Harry had gone under protest. She'd been trying to avoid being alone with Dominic, but that day it wasn't to prove possible. Harry drank too much wine and fell asleep in the bamboo-edged clearing where they were lounging in the shade. He left his wife and best friend to amuse themselves. She knew it was unwise to accept when Dominic suggested they climbed the pagoda to look at the view, but she went because she had changed that day as well.

The five-storied scarlet-and-gold tower was more than one hundred feet high, and each floor had a brightly gilded upward-curving roof with golden wind chimes hanging from the eaves. At the top there was a slender pinnacle that reached out of the valley toward the sky, and as she glanced up it seemed to move against the scattered white clouds.

Dominic held her hand as they climbed the steps to

the topmost balcony. The wind chimes played softly in the breeze, the scent of flowers filled the air, and the nearby waterfall splashed audibly down the hillside. Time seemed to stop, as if they'd crossed into another dimension where there was nothing to keep them apart.

He said her name, just her name, and it was as if he caressed her. He still held her hand, and she didn't resist as he drew her toward him. She knew it was wrong, but it was also more exciting and exhilarating than anything she'd ever known. She lifted her lips naturally to meet his in a kiss that began softly but soon became more insistent. There was no innocence, for it was the culmination of the intense emotion they'd suppressed for so long.

Desire tightened her breasts so her nipples pressed through her gown as she surrendered to the onslaught of erotic pleasure. He pressed her hips to his, and wild sensations sprang inside her as she felt how aroused he was. She was shameless and abandoned, and had no right to be because she was Harry's wife. But it was Dominic's virility that rose for her now, and his body she craved, not Harry's. If only she'd met this man first. If only.

Their mouths moved sensuously together as the kiss carried them away, but just as their passion reached the very brink of consummation, Harry called them from the foot of the staircase. The spell splintered into a million fragments and the air was suddenly chill on her skin. Remorse flooded accusingly over her, and when she pulled guiltily back from Dominic's embrace, she looked up to see shattered vows reflected in his gaze. *Her* shattered vows. She knew she'd never stop wanting him, but also that she'd never break the solemn promises she'd made at the altar. She belonged to Harry, and had to forget forever these few wild moments of summer madness.

Dominic had put his fingertips to her cheek, but she'd shaken her head. She'd blinked back tears as she left him to go down to Harry. She'd been widowed the very next day . . .

As her thoughts continued to move in the past, Dominic's voice intruded from the present. "Camilla? I asked you a question."

Her eyes flew to him. "I—I beg your pardon?"

"Apart from the pagoda, is there anywhere else de Marne might hide on the estate?"

She struggled to collect herself. "No. He must be at one of the inns, the pagoda isn't exactly warm and sheltered at this time of the year."

"De Marne has love to keep him warm," Dominic observed dryly.

His ironic tone reminded her how different he was from the man she'd kissed in the pagoda. She felt the sting of salt in her eyes as the sweet notes of the wind chimes echoed through her awareness from that lost summer day. Her conscience mocked her. Of all the fools on Fools' Day, you are by far the greatest, it scorned.

Suddenly she couldn't stay with him a moment longer. "You have your volume on falconry, my lord," she said in a choked voice, and then hurried from the room.

Chapter 11

Camilla didn't contribute much to the conversation during dinner, although her quietness wasn't particularly noticed because Sophie had so much to say. The czar's ward's mood had brightened considerably, and the change heightened her companions' suspicion that she not only knew William was somewhere nearby, but would also soon see him again. If this was so, and Mary was the lovers' messenger, Dominic had instructed his man Thomas to follow the maid when she left for the village.

Sophie's voice tinkled constantly in the elegant dining room, where the pale green walls were painted with white dragons and the table and chairs were richly embellished with bamboo and ivory. French windows opened into the adjoining conservatory, where a billiard table stood among the luxuriant tropical shrubs that flourished beneath the south-facing glass.

Sophie, who looked enchanting in a bluebell satin gown, revealed an unexpected talent for mimicry, especially when it came to mocking the Prince Regent, whose eccentricities made him an ideal target. She hadn't been at Carlton House for more than a few hours, but had observed him very sharply indeed, much to Dominic's amusement.

Camilla wished she could join in the humor, but couldn't shake off the uneasy memories that pervaded everything now Dominic was in the house again. The room was warm, but she felt cold in her thin jonquil silk gown. His closeness affected her, forcing her to recall the good times as well as the bad. She glanced at him as the meal progressed. The candlelight caught the jeweled pin in his lacy neckcloth, and shone with shades of purple on his indigo velvet coat. His eyes were lazily amused as he smiled at Sophie, and there was little sign of the hauteur and aloofness for which he had recently become known, nor did he seem in the least concerned to be beneath Sir Harry Summerton's roof once more.

The meal came to an end, but as Camilla and Dominic prepared to adjourn to the drawing room, Sophie held back. "Please may we play billiards?" she asked, glancing through into the conservatory.

Dominic was prepared to humor her. "As you wish, mademoiselle." He looked at Camilla. "Is that in order, my lady?"

"Certainly, although I will not join you. I—I wish to write to Elizabeth," she replied as Sophie went eagerly into the conservatory. She didn't want to write a letter at all, she merely saw an opportunity to avoid his company.

"Ah, yes, the loyal Lady Elizabeth," he murmured.

"She's a good friend."

His blue eyes were disdainful. "There are some things one is better off without, madam, and a friend like Lady Elizabeth Oxforth is one."

"I'm sure she feels the same toward you, sir."

"Oh, I don't doubt it, but then she has good reason to be uncomfortable where I'm concerned."

Irritation flashed through Camilla. "Yet another equivocal remark, sir? I wish you would either explain in full or stop doing it, for I'm getting tired of your continuous mysterious sniping toward Elizabeth, and indeed toward her brother. You're a guest who has been forced upon me, but that doesn't mean I'm obliged to put up with everything you choose to say or do."

"The noble martyr? Is that how you see yourself?" he murmured.

Color rushed into her cheeks. "Sarcasm is the lowest form of wit, sir."

"And hair shirts are the least becoming form of apparel, madam." With a cool nod, he went to join Sophie.

Camilla tossed a look of loathing after him, and then gathered her skirts to hurry up to the drawing room.

Dominic's lace-trimmed shirt was very white in the lamplight as he watched Sophie at the billiard table. He could see she was only pretending to have her mind on the game, for her glance was too frequently averted toward the darkness outside. He would have laid odds she was waiting for Mary to return from the village. The maid would cross the terrace outside the conservatory, and that was why Sophie had this sudden urge to play billiards.

At last he saw her pause as something caught her attention through the glass. Just as he expected, Mary's shadowy figure hurried past.

Sophie put her cue down suddenly. "I—I have a headache, Lord Ennismount."

"I'm sorry to hear that, mademoiselle."

"It is so bad I think I must lie down."

"Of course. Good night, mademoiselle."

"Good night, *milord.*"

He didn't follow when she hurried out, but chalked the tip of his cue and then took aim on one of the balls. The ivory chinked satisfyingly, and the ball rolled into the far pocket. He hummed to himself as he carefully potted each ball on the table, and he was just setting them all up again when he heard the step he'd been expecting behind him.

"Yes, Thomas?" He straightened and turned.

His man was dressed in a warm cloak and had hastily removed his hat. He was a little stout, with receding hair and a pointed nose, and he was out of breath. "I did everything you said, my lord. I followed the maid into the village and waited while she called on her family. When she left, she didn't take the same path as before, but went to a crossroad by the church. There's a hollow oak tree there, and she took out a note that had been hidden inside."

"There was no sign of de Marne himself?"

"No, my lord, just the note."

"Then what?"

"She came straight back here, and as soon as she got back Mamselle came to her."

"Was anything said?"

"Not really. Mamselle just seemed very excited to get the note. She didn't say who it was from or what it said. Then she went up to her room and Mary stayed in the kitchens to have a bite of supper before attending Lady Camilla and Mamselle later on."

"Thank you, Thomas, you've been a great help."

"My lord." Thomas wiped his forehead with a handkerchief.

Dominic smiled. "I see you aren't accustomed to so much exercise."

"I haven't walked so far since I was courting Betty Jenkins, my lord," Thomas replied with feeling.

"I can imagine. Well, your efforts tonight are appreciated, and I'll see you're rewarded for your pains, but in the meantime I wish you to continue keeping a close eye on Mary. I want to hear anything that might be pertinent."

"My lord."

"That will be all."

"Sir." Thomas bowed and withdrew.

Dominic put his cue back on the rack and turned to pick up his coat. He was thoughtful. Did the czar's defiant little ward intend to meet her lover tonight? Somehow he didn't think so, but there was always the chance. That being the case, he had no option but to warn Camilla things were already on the move.

As he donned the coat he found himself recalling another time when he'd done the same thing in this conservatory. It had been during the summer of Harry's disagreeable conduct, and then as now, he'd been whiling away the minutes at the billiard table. He was waiting for Camilla and Harry to return from calling upon the vicar of Summerton, when they were all to go for a picnic in the Chinese garden.

At last the open landau bowled along the drive, and he could see Camilla's blue parasol twirling as she sat at Harry's side. But it wasn't twirling lightheartedly, and the closer the landau drew, the more clearly he could see the strained look on her face. She wore a white muslin gown with a blue sash, and her dark hair was pinned up beneath a dainty blue silk hat.

Harry was unsmiling beside her. He'd flung himself on the seat, with one arm resting along the carriage door and the other lying idly behind his wife, and even from a distance the awkward atmosphere between them was almost tangible. Harry was to blame, as he had been all through the visit, and Camilla was being brought quite low on account of it. Dominic remembered his own growing contempt for his old friend, but then he had guessed what lay behind Harry's changed character.

The landau halted and Harry alighted to hold his hand out to his wife. The breeze tugged her hat as she stepped down, loosening her hairpins so much that she removed the hat altogether and allowed her dark curls to tumble down over her shoulders. Harry didn't respond to her quick smile, and her eyes were downcast as they proceeded into the house. Then the bitter past faded into oblivion again, taking the summer sunshine with it and leaving the night-darkened glass of the present.

Dominic's smile was ironic. "Deceit and deception, all is deceit and deception," he murmured, straightening his coat collar and then leaving the conservatory to go up to the drawing room. But as he reached the top of the staircase, Sophie emerged from her apartment.

She halted on seeing him. "Lord Ennismount, I was just coming down to see you."

"How is your headache, mademoiselle?"

She lowered her eyes. "It—it is still there, *milord*."

"I'm sure it will benefit from a good night's sleep."

"Yes, I'm sure it will too, and I was just going to

retire, but then I remembered I hadn't asked you something."

"How may I help you, mademoiselle?" he inquired.

"I would like to go for a ride in the park tomorrow morning."

"I see. Well, wouldn't it be more appropriate to ask Lady Camilla? After all, this is her house, and the horses are in her stables."

"If I ask her she will feel obliged to accompany me, but I like to ride alone. I was allowed to at St. Petersburg," Sophie added quickly.

Dominic doubted very much if the czar's ward, at the age of only thirteen or fourteen, which is what she had been when last in Russia, would have been permitted such liberty, but he didn't argue. "Very well, mademoiselle, I will ask Lady Camilla for you, but I'm certain it will be in order."

Sophie's lilac eyes brightened. "Oh, thank you, Lord Ennismount. Good night."

"Good night, mademoiselle."

"Please, will you call me Sophie? Lady Camilla does, and it is so much more friendly, *n'est-ce pas?*"

"As you wish, Sophie."

"*À demain, milord.*"

"Until tomorrow, Sophie."

He watched as she returned to her apartment. If she wished to ride alone in the park, he could only conclude she probably intended to meet de Marne then. Well, the czar's ward might plan an expedition on her own, but she'd be discreetly accompanied, for he and Camilla would follow at a distance. His decision made, he continued his way to the drawing room.

Chapter 12

Camilla finished her letter to Elizabeth just before Dominic left the conservatory.

Firelight flickered over the turquoise-and-gold drawing room as she held the sealing wax to a candle. The room was the most dazzling in a house of dazzling rooms. Wall panels of exquisite Chinese floral silk alternated with tall mirrors painted with the same flowery pattern, and light was provided by golden lanterns of exquisite workmanship. The dragon-decked grandfather clock chimed the hour as she pressed her ring into the pool of wax.

The only painting in the room was a full-length portrait of Harry. It hung above the porcelain Buddhas on the mantel, and was so lifelike it seemed he might step down from the canvas at any moment. The artist had caught him well, from the unruliness of his blond hair and tilt of his head, to the faint half-smile on his lips and the way he had of looking from slightly lowered eyes. There were times when the painted smile seemed about to become flesh and blood; it was one of those times now.

She suddenly felt as if the portrait were watching her. It was a strange sensation, and she looked up swiftly. Harry seemed to look back at her, but not with the charm and warmth for which she'd loved him so. Suddenly it was the day of the picnic again, and she and Harry had just come back from Summerton village, where their visit with the vicar had been almost embarrassingly marred by Harry's sourness and deliberate air of ennui. When they alighted from the landau they'd come straight up here to the drawing room to wait for Dominic to join them from his lonely game of billiards.

Harry stood by the sun-filled window tapping a folded newspaper against his thigh. She spoke to him, a lighthearted remark of no consequence, but he didn't bother to respond. Until that moment she'd been intent upon laughing him out of his sullen preoccupation, but now her smile died away. Why was he like this? What was wrong?

She went to him, slipping her arms around his waist from behind and resting her head against his shoulder. "Everything's all right, isn't it, Harry?"

"Why shouldn't it be?"

"I don't know, but you've hardly been good company since we arrived. No, it started before we left, for you were a sulky bear when we dined with Elizabeth."

"Was I? I couldn't say."

"Elizabeth noticed as well."

He didn't reply.

Perplexed, she took her arms away. "Please tell me what's wrong, Harry, for I can't stand things to be like this."

He turned. "Nothing's wrong."

"Then why are you so surly and bad-tempered all the time?" An alarming thought struck her. "Are you ill? Is that it? Because if you are, I wish you'd tell me!"

Remorse touched him for a moment and he put his hand swiftly to her cheek. "No, I'm not ill."

Her fingers closed anxiously over his. "This isn't fair, Harry. I'm your wife, and—"

"And nothing, sweetheart," he murmured, giving her an almost absentminded kiss on the cheek before moving away from the window to toss the newspaper on to the writing desk. He smiled then. "I'm sorry, Camilla, I don't mean to be a bear, it's just that I really didn't want to leave London this time."

"What is so interesting about London at the moment?"

"Oh, nothing particularly, I just had a hankering to stay in town, that's all."

"A hankering? Forgive me, Harry, but your bad mood would suggest a little more than that."

"That's all it is," he insisted.

"We can go back if you like," she offered.

He shook his head. "There's no need. We planned a long stay, and that's what we'll have."

"But—"

"We also have Dominic to consider, after all we *did* invite him," he reminded her.

"Dominic? But he won't care a fig if we change our plans. You know how easygoing he is about such things."

Harry studied her for a moment. "Do you find him attractive?" he asked suddenly.

Her heart stopped. "Attractive?" she repeated slowly, praying there was no shadow of guilt in her eyes. Had he guessed how much she'd always been drawn to Dominic?

"I'm told the fair sex find him irresistible."

"I'm sure some of them do. Why do you ask?" Were her cheeks red? Please, don't let them be.

"Because I think he admires you."

She gave a weak smile. "I—I'm flattered you think so, but I doubt it. To him I'm simply your wife." May I be forgiven such an untruth. Contrition cut through her, as if she'd done so very much more than silently yearn to be in Dominic's arms.

Harry reached out to take her hand then, pulling her swiftly toward him and putting his hand over her left breast. He caressed her through her gown, taking her nipple between his fingers and stroking it. She closed her eyes with pleasure, for he hadn't made love to her for days now, and she needed him. She also needed the reassurance that he still loved her . . .

Touching her excited him and he pressed her against his arousal, moving his hips slowly to heighten his pleasure. His eyes were dark, and a faint smile played on his lips. "No man can remain immune to you, my darling, and if Dominic held you like this now, I daresay he'd spread you over that writing desk."

"I want you, not Dominic," she whispered, trying to push all thought of Dominic from her mind. But she couldn't. It was wrong, but she wanted to be sexually intimate like this with Dominic . . .

Harry gave a low laugh. "But you've already had me, my darling. Don't you want to sample someone else?"

Her excitement subsided swiftly and she pulled back. "Don't say things like that, Harry."

"Why not? I find it erotic to think of you with someone else, very erotic indeed," he murmured, drawing her close again and lowering his lips to hers. At first it was a gentle kiss, teasing her back into response, but then it became rough. His mouth was harsh upon hers, and desire seemed to take him over so he didn't care how she felt. The hard shaft at his loins pushed forcefully against her, and his fingers tightened painfully over her breast.

Her breath caught and she tried to pull away, but he was too strong. She was frightened, for she'd never known him to be like this before. He began to maneuver her toward the desk. He was going to take her right here and now, when Dominic might come in at any moment! No, not that! Her struggles increased and at last she dragged herself free.

"Don't! You're hurting me!" she cried.

For a moment he seemed confused, as if her cry had awakened him. He ran his fingers nervously through his hair, and then he gave a rueful smile. "Forgive me . . ."

"I'm your wife, not some whore you've paid for a few minutes' carnal gratification!"

"I've said I'm sorry."

"Yes, and I trust you mean it. I don't know what's wrong with you at the moment, but I feel there's far more to your reluctance to leave London than you've admitted."

"There's nothing," he replied shortly, turning away again.

Before she could say anything else, the doors where flung open and Dominic came in. The atmosphere in the room must have been palpably strained, for the greeting died on his lips.

He glanced at Harry's back, and then looked at her. He smiled concernedly, and it was a smile that breached her damaged defenses. In this of all moments she was susceptible to his silent caring. She was vulnerable and neglected, and the fierce attraction she'd always felt toward him now surged to the fore.

But suddenly the sunshine of that day dimmed into candlelight again as Dominic's present-day footsteps approached the drawing room. She gave a start and turned toward the sound, for time might almost have overlapped. The doors were flung open and she couldn't help giving a small cry as he came in.

But there was no smile of gentle concern on his face now, instead he paused and looked curiously at her. "Are you all right?" he asked.

She stared at him, and then collected her wits. "I, er, didn't hear you coming, that's all."

"Perhaps I should sing a hymn next time," he said dryly, closing the doors.

She faced him. "It would seem the billiard table didn't hold much interest," she said.

"The czar's ward couldn't have cared less about billiards, she merely wished to be in the conservatory to see Mary return from the village." He explained what Thomas had told him.

Camilla was dismayed. "I wish I could think the note wasn't from William."

"So do I."

"Have you spoken to Sophie yet?"

"Not on this matter."

"But surely it would be better to confront her?"

"I've already said I want to catch them actually meeting."

"And if you don't catch them? Sophie's in our custody, we're responsible for looking after her, and that means seeing she's properly protected."

"I'm fully aware of that, which is why I've had second thoughts about the maid. I now think it will be better if she becomes our informant. I want you to tell her you expect to be told everything about Sophie's activities. It's time Mary was reminded where her true loyalties should lie."

Camilla nodded and looked away. "Very well."

"See you do it before we go out tomorrow."

"Go out?"

"Sophie wishes to go for a ride on her own in the park in the morning, and since she announced this desire after receiving the note, I think we can draw an obvious conclusion. You and I will be able to trail her, and so I took the liberty of saying I was sure you'd permit her to ride if she wished."

"It seems I have little choice."

"You have every choice, madam, for you can stay here and do your needlework if you so desire," he murmured.

The gulf between them was suddenly a chasm, and she couldn't help glancing at Harry's portrait.

Dominic noticed. "Remorse, remorse, and yet again remorse," he said coolly.

"I see it amuses you to taunt me."

"Amuses me? I don't find anything amusing in this. When will you stop pretending, Camilla? You can't forgive yourself for once toying with the notion of committing adultery. That's all there is to it!"

She recoiled furiously. "How dare you? I would *never* have committed adultery, least of all with you!"

"Now you're being childish," he replied acidly. "You and I both know how it was, and although you may not have slipped finally beyond redemption at the time, you came damned close. You were tempted and now must forever punish yourself in order to placate your damned conscience."

"I don't have to listen to this . . ." Snatching her skirts, she made to leave the room, but he barred her way.

"I'm tired of your self-inflicted guilt, madam, for it looms over reality like some great mythical monster. You and I did nothing, except steal a few kisses, but you behave as if we conducted a passionate and abandoned liaison that broke every marriage vow you uttered! Well, since you're eaten up inside over nothing, perhaps it's time to give your guilt something to feed on!"

"What do you mean?"

His eyes were piercing. "This is what I mean, madam," he said softly, and before she knew it he'd taken her into his arms. He allowed her no quarter as he kissed her. She struggled, but he held her too tightly, and she couldn't break free as she had from Harry because Dominic was in complete command of his senses. Resistance was futile, she could only submit.

Loathing seized her at first, but was soon followed by confusion. The blood began to flow more swiftly through her veins and her skin became warm and flushed as her flesh betrayed her. Her body yielded and she surrendered to the kiss, her lips parting to admit his tongue. Her dreams at the inn had told the truth. Nothing would ever change for her. The desire kindled in the earliest days still burned through her like a flame. She would live with her wanton shame, but, oh, God, how she hated him! How she hated herself!

Suddenly he thrust her away with a scornful smile.

"What price your conscience now, my lady?" he breathed.

Bitter tears stung her eyes as she struck him with all her might. The blow left an angry mark on his cheek, but still he smiled. "My, my, how desperately you try to pretend, but it doesn't wash with me, Camilla. You've always wanted me as much as I wanted you, and in spite of everything, you still feel the same."

"No!"

"Yes." Suddenly he took her by the shoulders and turned her to face Harry's portrait. "Do you hear the faint sound of laughter, my lady? I can, for I know how amused Harry would be if he knew how interminably foolish you are." He thrust her away and strode from the room.

A sob caught in her throat and she hid her face in her hands. She could still feel his lips over hers, and the beguiling warmth of unwilling desire. But as she tried to muster her hatred, it seemed she could indeed hear laughter. Harry's laughter.

Chapter 13

Camilla interrogated her maid first thing the following morning.

"Good morning, Mary," she said, sitting up in bed and pushing her untidy hair from her face.

"Good morning, my lady," Mary replied as she drew back the dusky blue velvet curtains so the morning sunlight flooded into the room.

Camilla got up to sit by the fire, where the warmth drew out the lingering fragrance of long-gone incense from the two burners on the hearth. She glanced at the maid. "Have you attended Mamselle yet, Mary?"

"Yes, my lady."

"I trust she's looking forward to riding on such a beautiful morning?"

"Yes, my lady," Mary said as she brought the customary cup of tea.

Camilla looked up into her eyes. "You've been betraying my trust, haven't you, Mary?" she said quietly.

The maid's breath caught. "Oh, no, my lady! I wouldn't do anything to—"

"But you have, Mary, you've been assisting Mam-

selle in her liaison with Lord de Marne. Well? It's
true, isn't it?"

"I . . ." Mary bit her lip. "Yes, my lady, but I've
only carried messages."

"Did you know Mamselle is to be betrothed to
someone other than Lord de Marne?"

Mary's eyes widened with dismay. "No, my lady,
she just said she was being cruelly parted from the
gentleman she loved with all her heart. She told me
Lord de Marne was all that was suitable, but that Lady
Cayne disapproved so much she'd beaten her."

Camilla stared and then gave an incredulous laugh.
"She said what? That Lady Cayne *beat* her?"

"Yes, my lady."

"Mamselle has lied to you in order to gain your
help, Mary," Camilla said, thinking privately that if
there was one thing Sophie Arenburg *did* deserve it
was a sound beating.

Tears filled Mary's eyes. "I—I'm very sorry, my
lady."

"So you should be."

"What will you do, my lady? Am I to be dis-
missed?"

"It would be no more than you deserve."

A sob choked Mary's voice. "I—I was sorry for
her, my lady. I really believed she'd been beaten at
Ennismount House, and I wanted to help her. I didn't
think I was being disloyal to you."

"I'll consider keeping you on provided you tell me
everything you know. What happened before we left
London?"

"Lord de Marne didn't go to Scotland, he tried to
see Mamselle the first night she came to you. He
nearly got caught.'

Camilla's lips parted. "Are you saying Lord de Marne was the burglar?"

"Yes, my lady, then he came back to Cavendish Square the next morning, when it was foggy. I was just taking him a note from Mamselle when you came into the room."

Camilla thought back. Sophie had been standing by the window, and said the maid had gone for tea, but Mary came back without any. "Go on, Mary."

"The note asked Lord de Marne to come to the kitchen door that night, when everyone had gone to bed. Mamselle hoped by then she'd know if she could come here with you, and which way we'd travel. She wanted to see him during the journey, when we stopped at the Cross Keys."

How right Dominic had been. Camilla drew a slow breath. "Lord de Marne was in the kitchens when I went down, wasn't he?"

Mary nodded. "Yes, my lady. He and Mamselle were drinking chocolate when we heard you calling. He left very quickly, and all the night air came in when the door jammed open for a few moments. That's why it felt so cold."

"So they arranged to meet at the Cross Keys?"

"Yes, although Lord de Marne wasn't happy about it, he said it was too risky, but Mamselle insisted. Anyway, in case they couldn't meet there after all, they had a plan for contacting each other from here. I told them about the hollow tree in the village, and Lord de Marne said he'd leave a note there to say where he was staying. I—I went for the note last night when I went to see my family."

"What did it say?"

Mary hung her head. "I don't know, my lady. It was

sealed, and Mamselle threw it on the fire as soon as she'd read it."

"Do you know where Lord de Marne is?"

"No, my lady."

"Is that the truth?"

"Yes, my lady."

"Is there anything else I should be told?"

"No, my lady, except that Mamselle is going to meet his lordship during her ride this morning. That's why she didn't want anyone to accompany her."

"We thought as much," Camilla murmured.

Mary looked imploringly at her. "I—I've told you everything, my lady, truly I have. Please don't dismiss me, I'll never do anything like this again, I swear I won't."

"I'll forgive you this time, Mary, for Mamselle deceived you into helping her and I know how convincing an actress she can be, but you aren't to say anything to her about this conversation. Is that understood?"

"Yes, my lady."

"And if you find out more, you're to tell me immediately."

"I will, my lady."

"Believe me, in many ways I have every sympathy with Mamselle and Lord de Marne, for I have no doubt they're truly in love, but they're both promised elsewhere, and while those other matches exist neither of them has any business doing what they're doing, especially when high politics and the Czar of Russia are involved. Have I made myself crystal clear?"

Mary swallowed. High politics and the Czar of Russia? "Yes, my lady."

"Very well, I'll say no more on the matter. Now

then, I'll require my pink gingham for breakfast, but afterward I'll need my riding habit."

"Yes, my lady."

"And the fact that Mamselle isn't the only one who'll be riding this morning should not be transmitted to her."

"No, my lady."

It was almost time for Sophie's ride, and Camilla and Dominic waited in their separate apartments for her to set off. Camilla wore her emerald green riding habit and black top hat, and she stood at her bedroom window to look out at the estate she loved so much.

Summerton Park was enchanting at every time of year, but perhaps looked its best on a bright spring day. She glanced toward the Chinese garden. It had been created about a quarter of a mile from the house, where a stream cascaded down the steep wooded side of the valley to join the river. The shining water tumbled past rocks, bamboo thickets, and pink-and-white blossoms, but it was the elegant pagoda halfway up the garden that dominated everything. She could see the golden wind chimes, and knew they'd be playing softly in the breeze, just as they had the day she and Dominic had climbed to the top.

She looked away. Why did everything always come back to Dominic? For two long years she'd tried to keep him from her thoughts, but now he was there all the time, and the kiss he'd forced upon her in the drawing room had increased the pain tenfold, because even while she hated him, she desired him as well. She faced two ways, and was being torn in both directions at once.

At last she heard Sophie hurry past her door, and waited until the light footsteps died away before emerging to follow her. She met Dominic at the top of the staircase, and there was an awkward moment as thoughts of the kiss beset her again. She avoided his eyes as she accepted his arm, and neither of them spoke as they descended to the entrance hall. They left the house by way of the kitchens, crossing the high-walled vegetable garden to the wicket gate that opened into the stableyard. There they halted because Sophie had yet to leave.

She waited impatiently by the clock tower as a groom saddled a chestnut mare for her. She wore a mustard yellow riding habit, and her blond hair was pinned up beneath a jaunty plumed hat. There was no mistaking her unease as she glanced back toward the house, but she couldn't see through the wicket gate.

There was a sudden clatter of hooves and a shout as another groom led a large and very mettlesome roan stallion into the yard from the paddock. It was a difficult animal, and tossed its head and capered as it tried to loosen the man's hold on the leading rein.

Camilla froze as she saw the horse, for it was the image of the one Harry had ridden when he died, and seeing it being led like that took her back to the day she'd first seen that other stallion. It was before Harry had changed so much, and before the fateful visit to Summerton Park. The day had commenced with a ride she and Harry took in Hyde Park. They encountered Dominic on his way to the horse auctions at Tattersall's, and he told Harry about a particularly fine but supposedly unmanageable roan thoroughbred he wished to examine. She could still see Harry's disbelieving grin, and hear his voice.

"Unmanageable? Oh, come now!"

"So I'm told." Dominic's gaze moved briefly toward her, and he smiled.

Her pulse quickened, and her gloved hands tightened over the reins, for his smiles weakened her resolve so much.

Harry looked quizzically at him. "If the animal's unmanageable, why are you keen to see it?"

"Just idle curiosity."

"You never do anything out of idle curiosity."

"Don't credit others with your own deviousness, Harry. If I say it's idle curiosity, then that's what it is."

"I still say you have an ulterior motive. What is it, eh? Is the nag the swiftest thing on hoof? Is that it?"

"I've no idea if it goes or not."

Harry's eyes had sharpened now. "You don't fool me."

"Harry, there's truly nothing to read into this. I haven't got any inside information, I've just heard about the horse and since I'm at loose ends thought I'd toddle along to take a peek."

Harry wasn't convinced. "You old rogue, you're trying to pull the wool over my eyes! Hasn't Charley Curzon challenged you to a race? Yes, I remember now, there's a tidy heap of guineas resting on whether you can find a nag to outrun his!"

Dominic sighed. "You're wrong, Harry. Charley Curzon's challenge is with Dick Painswick, not me."

"I've still got a fancy to see this brute. What d'you say, Camilla? Shall we tag along? I know ladies don't usually go to Tattersall's, but you can be the exception, eh?"

She didn't particularly want to, but at the same time part of her wished to be with Dominic. "I suppose so . . ."

Dominic shrugged at Harry. "As you wish, but you're totally wrong about this."

And so they'd been in Tattersall's yard when the roan was led out. A stir passed through the crowd of fashionable gentlemen, for it was a particularly beautiful animal, with a magnificent head and neck and perfect action. But the look in its eye told of a mean nature and it was clearly dangerous, but Harry was still convinced Dominic was up to something.

He watched as the horse was led up and down. "Admit you intend to buy, Dominic," he said at last. "You have an agent here somewhere who's going to bid for you."

"You're wrong," Dominic said again, a hint of irritability entering his voice.

"Then you won't object if I bid."

She was dismayed. Buy such a monster? "Oh, no, Harry! Just look at how spiteful it is!"

"Dominic knows something and I intend to steal his thunder."

Dominic sighed. "Why don't you listen to me, Harry? I'm *not* after the horse, I'm merely curious to see it, so for God's sake stop being such a damned fool! What are you going to do with such a vicious nag?"

But Harry only grinned and raised his hand the moment the bidding began.

Another gentleman was keen to acquire the horse, and Harry became more and more convinced that he was Dominic's agent. Each time the other man put in a bid Harry raised the price, until there were astonished whispers in the yard as the incredible sum of three thousand guineas was reached. Then the other man shook his head, and to her unutterable dismay, the horse was knocked down to Harry, who grinned triumphantly at Dominic.

"Not your agent, eh? Ha! Now we'll see!"

Dominic exhaled slowly. "You've just wasted three thousand guineas."

"I don't think so," Harry said, pushing his way through the crowds to examine his acquisition more closely.

She turned angrily to Dominic. "Why did you have to tell him about the horrid creature?"

"I wasn't to know he'd do this."

She lowered her eyes. "No, I suppose not," she murmured.

"I wouldn't do a thing like that, and you know it."

She was contrite. "Forgive me."

That had been then. Later, when Harry lay dead, she wondered a great deal about the whole incident. Had Dominic mentioned the horse in all innocence? Had he known Harry wouldn't be able to resist purchasing it? But the darkest question of all was whether or not he'd hoped Harry would perish trying to ride the horse? Had he wanted Harry out of the way so that she became free? She closed her eyes now as this other roan horse was led across the Summertown Park stableyard.

Dominic's cold voice intruded. "Do you intend to stand there in a daze, or are we going to follow Sophie?"

Her eyes flew open again.

He nodded toward the yard. "Our little bird flew off while you were having a leisurely daydream. She only left at a slow trot but I still think it would be prudent to follow, don't you?"

"There was nothing leisurely about my thoughts,

sir, nor could they be even remotely described as day-dreams," she replied sharply, as he ushered her through the wicket gate.

Two saddled horses were led from the stalls where they'd been kept hidden while Sophie was around. Dominic quickly helped Camilla to mount, but as she gathered the reins her glance moved once more to the roan, and she spoke to the groom leading it.

"How is that horse here? I don't remember it."

"Mr. Rowlands purchased it two days ago, my lady. It's the one he told you about before you left for London."

Rowlands was her head groom, and had indeed mentioned a good stallion that could be bought to replace one she'd just lost. She'd never have agreed to its acquisition if she'd known it was a roan. "I see, well please inform Rowlands that I wish it to be sold again as quickly as possible. Any replacement he then purchases must not be roan, is that clear?"

"Yes, my lady."

Dominic mounted and looked at her. "You're transparent at times, madam," he said softly.

"And you, sir, are opaque to a fault."

"Are you still trying to convince yourself?"

"I need no convincing, sir, I *know*."

He gave a disdainful smile. "I suppose you harbor a suspicion that I was somehow responsible for this acquisition as well?"

"You may not have had anything to do with it this time, sir, but you certainly did last time!"

"I didn't twist Harry's arm to make him bid, he chose to do it because he thought he was outsmarting me. I didn't have an agent at that auction, nor did I have the slightest intention of acquiring that four-legged demon. It was all in Harry's mind, and has remained in yours ever since. Now then, we have a quarry to run to ground." He kicked his heels and urged his horse out of the yard.

Chapter 14

Sophie rode slowly along the drive, but where it climbed toward the north lodge and Summerton village, she struck away to the south to follow the river toward the beechwood that closed the vista of the park.

Riding behind with Dominic, Camilla watched her vanish among the trees. Where was she going? If she was simply following the river, she'd soon leave the park by the south lodge bridge on to the Malmesbury road, and whichever direction she took then would take her to other villages and byroads, as well as various gentlemen's residences and villas.

Dominic knew this as well. "We must see which way she goes at the bridge," he said, urging his horse on.

Birdsong was deafening in the woods, and the air was sweet with the scent of new leaves. Lacework shadows dappled the ground as the sun shone down through the branches high overhead, and every clearing was filled with the budding bluebells that in a few weeks would transform the woods to a haze of color to match the sky. There was no sign of Sophie now, but her horse's hoofprints were clearly visible in the soft earth along the riverbank.

The end of the woods appeared ahead, and the rolling Cotswold countryside beyond. Smoke curled idly up from the lodge chimney, and the river narrowed and deepened as it passed beneath the elegant stone bridge by the gates from the highway. Dominic and Camilla were so intent upon trying to spot Sophie somewhere along the road that they didn't see her closer to them than that; on the bridge itself, to be exact. She'd dismounted and was leaning on the parapet to watch the river as it swept beneath her. She raised her head to smile at them and wave, and they realized she knew she was being trailed.

They exchanged glances, for whatever they'd expected if they were caught following her, it wasn't a warm greeting.

She straightened as they reached the bridge. "*Bonjour, milord,* Lady Camilla. I did not know you wished to ride as well. It is a lovely day, *n'est-ce pas*?"

Camilla felt a little foolish as she managed a weak smile. "Yes, it is. We thought your idea of a ride was excellent and decided to do the same. We, er, didn't realize you'd come this way."

"I just followed the river." Sophie didn't seem in the least perturbed by their arrival, and certainly didn't glance around as if she feared William would appear at any moment and give the game away. She smiled at Camilla. "You are most fortunate to have an estate as beautiful as this, Lady Camilla."

"Yes, I am." Camilla caught Dominic's eyes and he gave a barely perceptible shrug, for he was as mystified as she, but the silently exchanged glance confirmed they both still felt certain a tryst had been the object of the exercise.

A light breeze rippled the surface of the river and Sophie shivered suddenly. "Oh, it is a little colder than it was. Shall we go back now?"

Camilla nodded. "Yes, of course."

Dominic dismounted to assist Sophie into the saddle again, but as she gathered the reins he noticed how she looked briefly toward some chimneys rising above a copse about a quarter of a mile along the road. He gave no sign of having noticed anything, and remounted to accompany the two women back to the house. But as they rode back through the woods, he suddenly reined in.

"Forgive me, ladies, but I have a fancy to ride a little more. I trust you won't mind?"

Sophie shook her head. "No, of course not, Lord Ennismount."

Camilla searched his face, sensing that something was up. "As you wish, my lord."

He turned his horse's head and rode away, striking off at a tangent as if he had no thought at all of returning to the south lodge, but the moment he was out of their sight, he made his way back to the bridge. Within a few minutes he was approaching the house hidden among the trees. The elegant wrought-iron gates stood directly on to the road, and the gravel drive curved away between rhododendrons that in summer were heavy with magenta blooms.

It was a scene he remembered only too well, for the last time he'd come here he'd been following Harry. It was the day after the picnic, a humid afternoon with thunderclouds burgeoning on the horizon, and from time to time the approaching storm was audible in the distance. Camilla was visiting a sick friend in Tetbury for a few hours, and Harry, who as yet didn't realize his friend had grown suspicious, had set off on horseback to come here the moment his wife departed. No one realized then that Harry and Camilla would never see each other again.

That far-off day returned now as Dominic stared along the drive. The bright spring morning became indistinct, and the growl of bygone thunder echoed beyond the horizon. Sound was accentuated, from the calls of a peacock on the hidden lawns to the rattle of the pony and trap that had driven past a few moments before. The rhododendrons were in full bloom along the drive, and the gates stood open.

On that day he'd kicked his heel and ridden through, and he did so again as past and present became inexorably entwined. He moved his horse slowly along the drive of April 1814, but it was the summer of 1812 he saw. He rode slowly, praying he was wrong about Harry's reason for coming here, but all the signs pointed to the contrary. Suddenly the rhododendrons sloped away from the drive as the grounds opened out into neatly tended lawns where the peacocks he'd heard could be seen strutting beneath the fronds of weeping willows. At the far end of the lawns stood the house itself, a small symmetrical mansion with a hipped roof and stone-faced windows.

Harry was dismounting in front of the house. For a moment it seemed no one in the house knew he'd arrived, but then the door opened and a fair-haired woman in a geranium silk gown emerged. She was very beautiful, and her joy was manifest as she ran into Harry's arms. They embraced passionately, their lips searing together in a kiss that could only lead to consummation the moment the door of the house closed behind them. Harry's hand slid to clasp her breast through the thin stuff of her gown, and she threw her head back so he could kiss her throat.

Thunder growled lazily across the heavens and the air became almost claustrophobic as the lovers went into the house. A groom came to take Harry's horse, and the watcher from the drive gazed up toward the second-floor windows of the house. Behind one of those windows, Camilla's adulterous husband was betraying her with his mistress.

A flock of rooks rose noisily from the trees, and suddenly it was the present again as Dominic stared past unkempt lawns toward a closed and shuttered house. There were no peacocks and gleaming panes now; the house was deserted and weeds grew in the drive.

Snatching his concentration back to the matter in hand, he glanced around for some sign of William, but everything was quiet. Dismounting, he led his horse out of sight among the rhododendrons and tethered it before making his way circuitously to the rear of the house. If Sophie Arenburg's lover was here, he was about to be caught.

Quietly he entered the small stableyard and examined each stall in turn, but there was no horse, and no sign of one having been there recently. Frowning, he searched the coach house as well, but the weeds growing in front of the doors hadn't been disturbed. He glanced at the house again. Everything was very quiet, and somehow he felt there was no one here but himself, but he had to check.

He moved to the kitchen door, but it was bolted on the inside, as was the side entrance. Just as he was

considering forcing one of them, he noticed a sash
window that hadn't been tightly closed. He found a
stick that fitted the gap and managed to flick the lock
aside to raise the window, then he climbed over the
sill into the red-tiled passage beyond.

It was very cold in the house, and he could smell
damp. Cobwebs swathed the ceiling and walls, and a
mouse scuttled toward a hole in the skirting. The passage ended with a door that made barely a sound as he
pushed it open. Beyond it lay a shadowy hall where
the chandeliers had been removed, leaving only ropes
dangling from the high ceiling. His reflection moved
in a wall mirror as he crossed to the foot of the
ghostly white marble staircase.

Suddenly he heard a scuffling sound from the next
floor. Someone was up there! He ascended quickly
and paused at the top to listen again. The sound was
still there. Wide passages led away on either side, but
he realized the noises were coming from the main
bedroom, directly opposite the staircase.

Taking a deep breath he flung the door open expecting to catch William unawares, but instead terrified wings fluttered frantically into his face. He tried
to protect his eyes, but then whatever it was flew past
into the abyss of the hall. He whirled about in time to
see it was only a pigeon. He gave a relieved laugh.
Dear God, what had he imagined it was? A winged
demon? A vengeful wraith?

Taking a deep breath, he glanced around the empty
bedroom where he knew Sir Harry Summerton had
often made love to his paramour. The furniture had
gone, but he could see where the canopied bed once
stood against the wall because its silhouette was
marked on the faded rose silk.

A nerve flickered at his temple. He'd despised Harry's memory for so long now that he almost felt nothing. The sighs and sweet sensuous sounds of the past tried to reach out to him, but he was immune. This was only one place where Harry had betrayed his wife with his mistress. And *still* Camilla cherished his memory! Turning on his heel, he returned to the staircase, and as he descended he could still hear the pigeon flapping helplessly against the ceiling as it tried to find a way out.

He rode back to Summerton Park as if the hounds of hell were behind him, just as he'd ridden back that other day. On that occasion he'd confronted Harry in the stables while a thunderstorm raged overhead; today the sky was blue and the sun was shining as he simply handed his horse over to a waiting groom and went into the house.

Camilla heard him cross the hall, and hurried out from the library. "I—I must speak with you."

He halted, and for a moment couldn't face her. But at last he turned, forcing a brief smile. "Yes?"

"In the library, it's more private."

"What is it?" he asked as she closed the library door behind them.

"Sophie *did* know we were following her. Mary came to me a short while ago. It seems Sophie caught a glimpse of us and so waited deliberately at the bridge."

"Well, we guessed as much."

"There's more. She was prepared for the possibility, and so she had another note with her which she hid on the bridge parapet just before we rode out of the woods. She told Mary that William was actually watching us from somewhere close by, and would have retrieved the note the moment we left."

He was incredulous. "Are you saying de Marne was there all the time?"

"Mary says so."

"Do we know yet where he's actually staying?"

"No."

He gave an angry sigh. "Do we at least know what Sophie's note said?"

"No, we don't. Sophie didn't tell Mary."

"Are we really expected to believe that? If Sophie told Mary so much, I'm very skeptical indeed that she didn't say everything," he replied scornfully.

"I think it's the truth. You see, when Sophie didn't volunteer anything about what she'd written, Mary made the mistake of asking her. Mary's afraid she aroused Sophie's suspicions. Anyway, nothing more was said."

Resignedly he tossed his gloves and riding crop on to a table, and then counted the adverse points on his fingers. "So we now have three things to contend with. One, de Marne is still waiting his moment in some hidey-hole, two, Sophie is well and truly on her guard, and three, we have absolutely no idea at all what her next move is to be."

"I'm afraid so."

"Then we'll just have to be more hawkish than ever, and Mary will certainly have to keep us minutely informed."

"She will, I'm sure."

"I wish I'd never heard of Sophie Arenburg, and that's a fact."

Camilla went to the window. "I feel the same, but we've managed to acquire responsibility for her."

"I had her foisted upon me, you must have been moonstruck to volunteer."

She smiled a little. "Possibly." She glanced at him. "Where did you go when you left Sophie and me?"

"Just for a ride," he replied evasively.

She searched his face and knew he was lying. "Dominic, if you know something, I'd prefer it if you told me."

For the space of a heartbeat he was tempted to tell her everything, if only to ease his own load, but as he saw the earnest look in her eyes, he knew he still couldn't. He had to leave her with her illusions. God rot the soul of dear departed Harry!

"I don't know anything, Camilla. I thought perhaps de Marne might be in a house I remembered, but it was deserted." He went to the door, and then looked back at her. "How remiss we've both been, my lady, so far forgetting our feud as to address each other by first names."

She lowered her eyes and he went out, but paused again on the other side of the door. He didn't want to hurt her, but he felt as taut as bowstring. Sooner or later the arrow had to fly, and when it found its mark Lady Camilla Summerton's treasured memories would be shattered. But so would his own dreams.

Chapter 15

In her dreams that night Camilla was with Harry again. They were making love in the bed where she slept now, and their lips burned passionately together as their pleasure intensified. But then his mouth became harsh and cruel as he thought only of himself. Her joy was obliterated by the savagery of his selfish thrusts, but she couldn't cry out her pain because his lips were forced so imperatively over hers. He was stifling her, stopping her very breath! She tried to pull away, but he was too strong.

Fear replaced ecstasy, and she began to struggle. The more she struggled, the more she was constrained into subjection, but then she realized she wasn't asleep anymore. She was wide awake, and a hand was clamped over her mouth as someone held her down!

"In God's name be still, Camilla!" Dominic hissed.

She froze, and stared up at him. He was fully dressed, and obviously hadn't been to bed at all.

He kept his hand over her mouth. "Are you going to be quiet?" he asked softly.

Slowly she nodded, and he took his hand away. "That's better."

She sat up fearfully, clutching the bedclothes to her throat. "Why are you here? What do you want?

"Not for what you appear to think. Sophie's up and about when she shouldn't be. I've been watching from the room opposite her apartment, and heard the moment she opened her door. She's just gone downstairs. Be quick, or we'll lose her." He thrust her cloak into her hands.

Collecting her scattered thoughts, Camilla slipped from the bed. His glance lingered on her legs, then he looked at her face. "I'm consumed with curiosity as to the nature of your dreams a moment or so ago," he murmured, remembering how sensuously she'd moaned in her sleep before he'd awakened her.

She flushed, but he didn't see as he went to the window and held the curtain aside to look out. It was a cold moonlit night, and the terrace was clearly visible below. "I have a sixth sense she'll go to the Chinese garden," he murmured. "There she is now! She's just crossing the terrace from the conservatory."

Camilla hastily put on her little ankle boots and joined him in time to see Sophie's cloaked figure fleeing down the terrace steps to the parterre. Dominic smiled as he saw which way she went across the grass. "It's the Chinese garden all right, and that has to mean the pagoda," he muttered, hurrying Camilla toward the door.

It was a cloudless night, and bitterly cold. The landscape sparkled with frost, and the park might have been fashioned from silver. Owls hooted in the woods and a vixen shrieked from somewhere toward the village as they followed Sophie swiftly across the grounds. The bell of Summerton church sounded. It was two o'clock.

Camilla was quite out of breath when they at last reached the edge of the Chinese garden. The pagoda pierced the starry heavens, its wind chimes silent on such a still night, but the splash of the cascading stream carried clearly as they paused beneath an almond tree that was weighed down with blossoms. They could see Sophie making her way up beside the waterfall, following the winding stone path that led to the foot of the pagoda.

Suddenly she hesitated and glanced directly toward them. They were well hidden, but Dominic instinctively drew Camilla farther back beneath the almond tree. Sophie continued to stare in their direction, and Camilla's heart began to quicken. Had she realized they were there again? But then Sophie hurried up the steps, and Dominic held a branch aside to watch for a moment before he and Camilla emerged.

Petals showered over her as he released the branch. "Come on," he said, catching her hand and leading her toward the steps. His fingers were warm in spite of the bitterly cold night, and she was very conscious of his touch, especially since in a moment they'd pass the hollow fringed with bamboo, where the picnic had taken place.

She averted her eyes, but she could still see Harry lying asleep on the grass, and Dominic, so charming and irresistible as he persuaded her to go to the pagoda with him. They'd gone hand in hand up this path, just as they were doing now . . . Guilt had walked with her on that day, for she'd known exactly what she was doing. If Harry hadn't awoken and called . . .

The memory was so sharp now that she snatched her hand away from Dominic's, but breaking the contact didn't absolve her of responsibility for the past. She'd gone more than willingly into the arms of her husband's best friend, and the unfulfilled passion had preyed upon her conscience ever since. Perhaps it would do so forever.

Sophie reached the pagoda entrance and went inside. Dismayed, Camilla caught Dominic's arm. "The door is supposed to be locked because the stairs are dangerous! We must stop her!"

He stared at her for a second, and then began to run toward the pagoda. He called, and his voice echoed around the garden until it was lost in the noise of the water, but Sophie didn't reappear.

Camilla hurried after him, but as they ran the final few yards to the entrance, Sophie suddenly came out. Her hands were pressed to her mouth and her eyes were large and round. She gave a cry and burst into tears when she saw them.

"Oh, Lady Camilla! Lord Ennismount! William is dead!"

"Dear God," Dominic breathed and dashed inside, where he found William lying among the shattered fragments of the banister and handrail that had given way when he'd climbed to the floor above. Dominic knelt down to feel his pulse.

Sophie watched anxiously, and hysteria suddenly seized her. "Oh, William! William! What shall I do now? What shall I do now?"

Camilla put her arms around her, afraid to offer words of comfort in case Sophie's worst fears were realized.

Dominic looked up. "It's all right, Sophie, he's not dead, he just knocked himself out when he fell."

But Sophie was beyond reason. Sob after sob rose uncontrollably in her throat and Camilla had to shake her. "Sophie! Listen to me! William isn't dead!"

The girl's breath caught, and she stared at her.

Camilla spoke more gently. "William isn't dead," she said again.

Tears filled Sophie's eyes. "You are telling the truth?"

"Of course I am." ·

"Oh, Lady Camilla!" Sophie gave her a quick hug and then hastened over to William. She knelt down and took his head to cradle it in her lap. "Oh, William! William! Speak to me, please!"

Dominic put a warning hand on her shoulder. "Have a care, for we don't know if he has any broken bones."

William groaned and began to stir, then his eyes opened. He gazed up into Sophie's anxious face. "Sophie . . ."

"Oh, William, *mon âme, mon coeur* . . ." She bent to smother his face with kisses.

Dominic looked at William's pale face. "Can you move your head?"

"I—I think so . . ."

William managed to turn his head from side to side, and Dominic gave him a wry glance. "Well, at least you haven't broken your idiotic neck."

"I'm sorry to disappoint you," William replied, but then winced as he tried to move his leg. "My ankle . . . !"

"Let me have a look." Dominic carefully tried to pull William's boot off, but the injured man gave a cry of pain.

"Dear God, no!"

Sophie's tender heart ached for him, and fresh tears filled her lilac eyes as she stroked his hair and whispered lovingly.

Dominic inspected the boot. "I'm afraid this will have to be cut off when we get you back to the house," he warned.

"But Hoby made them!" William protested.

"Hard luck," Dominic answered unfeelingly, and then straightened to look up at the broken banister. "You're fortunate it happened before you'd gone too far, a little higher and you might not have survived the fall. As to the consequences if Sophie had been the one to fall . . ."

"I'd never have allowed her to climb the stairs, I could see they weren't all they should be," William replied.

"Then more fool you for going up them at all!" Dominic replied trenchantly.

"Thanks," William answered offendedly.

"You don't expect sympathy, do you? You gave your word you'd go to Scotland and stay away from Sophie, but here you are."

"It's the only time in my life I've broken my word."

"Correction, it's at least the second time."

William looked at him in puzzlement. "Second?"

"You gave your word to Alice Penshill, didn't you? Or has that now slipped your mind completely?" Without waiting for William to reply, Dominic got to his feet and turned to Camilla. "Can you take Sophie back to the house and then have some men bring a stretcher?"

"Yes, of course."

"I think we can be reasonably sure the ankle is his only injury, so is there someone in Summerton who sets bones? I seem to remember the blacksmith . . . ?"

"Jem Clayton? Yes, I'll send for him."

She nodded and put her hand on Sophie's shoulder. "Come on, we'll go back to the house."

But Sophie shook her head. "I wish to stay with William, Lady Camilla."

"It's better that you come to the house with me."

"No!" St. Petersburg surged to the fore.

Dominic's patience finally snapped, and he seized her hand and dragged her to her feet. "Do as you're told, miss!" he said shortly, steering her out into the night.

"You cannot do this! I am the czar's ward!" she cried furiously.

"Czar's ward or not, I'll put you over my damned knee if you defy me any more! I'm sick to death of your conduct, which has certainly not been that of a lady, and which I'm sure you don't really wish the czar and the grand duchess to hear about. Well, I'm now of a mind to tell them *exactly* how disreputably you've behaved, and I'm also greatly tempted to spill the beans to the Earl of Highnam."

Sophie gasped. "No!"

"Give me one good reason why not."

"Because it happened when I was under your protection! Because I will say all sorts of things about the Prince Regent, the government, and—"

"Enough! Just think about the consequences to your own reputation, mademoiselle. If you wish to be regarded as no better than you should be, then so be it!"

Sophie's face went pale in the moonlight, and without another word she began to hurry away down the path.

Camilla gazed after her and then looked reproachfully at him. "Did you have to be quite so harsh? She's very upset about William, and—"

"I'm not in any mood for your bleeding heart, Camilla. That young woman chose the wrong moment to adopt her Romanov arrogance!"

"Romanov? So she *is* the czar's—?"

"Leave it, Camilla, for I really haven't the patience right now. I'm tired of this whole damned business, so just go after her and see she's all right, then keep her out of my way!"

She nodded, but then hesitated. "I—I think I'll have to send for Elizabeth," she said.

"Whatever for?"

"She should be here."

"Leave her in London," he replied shortly.

"I promised I'd send for her if anything untoward happened, and this is definitely untoward."

His eyes were cool in the moonlight. "I'd prefer it if you didn't send for her, but I can't stop you."

"No, you can't."

His lips twisted angrily. "There have been many times when I should have prevailed with you, Camilla, and the one that comes to mind most clearly of all was the last occasion we were here at this pagoda. I should have made you mine then, and to hell with your conscience and with Sir Harry Bloody Summerton!" Suddenly he put his hand to her chin, pinching with his fingers as he made her look at him. "I vow this, madam, if there's a third occasion when you and I find ourselves here, I'll finish what was so rudely interrupted before. Now get away from here and attend to your chaperonely duties!" He thrust her roughly away and then went back to William.

Shaken by his suppressed fury, and trembling with more than just the cold, Camilla gazed after him for a moment before gathering her skirts to follow Sophie.

Chapter 16

William had spent the previous night in a barn, an experience that hadn't permitted much comfort or rest, so that when his ankle had been attended to, and he was warm and comfortable, he immediately fell into a deep sleep.

But if he felt relaxed enough to sleep, Sophie most certainly didn't. Dominic's harsh words at the pagoda seemed to have at last made her realize the extent of her transgression. She paced anxiously up and down in the candlelit drawing room, twisting her handkerchief in her hands as all the worst possible consequences reared their ugly heads in the shadows all around. What if Dominic told the grand duchess what had been going on? What if the czar should learn about it, and cast his disobedient ward off? What if William should bow to his father's wishes, and marry Lord Penshill's daughter? What would happen to Sophie Arenburg then?

Dominic's intentions were not yet apparent, for as soon as William was taken care of, he'd retired to his own apartment without saying anything more, but there was no mistakening his anger with the young lovers. Camilla had no idea what he meant to do, but her own decision to write to Elizabeth remained unchanged. She sat at the writing desk in the drawing room, trying to compose a letter that wouldn't cause William's anxious sister any undue alarm, but Sophie's restlessness made it difficult to concentrate. In the end Elizabeth was merely informed that William had hurt his ankle at Summerton Park and wished to see her. It wasn't strictly true, of course, for William hadn't expressed any desire to see his sister, but Camilla felt it was the best way to break the unwelcome news that the future Earl of Highnam had put matters in jeopardy by breaking his word. She wished she could add that all was well, but that would have been a patent untruth.

At last Sophie's agitation proved too much. "Sophie, if you don't sit down I vow I'll go to my apartment as well and leave you to it!" she said, holding the sealing wax to the candle.

Sophie turned anxiously. "Oh, no, Lady Camilla, please do not do that. I—I could not bear to be on my own now."

"You've lied and taken advantage so much that I'm quite tired of you, and I'm certainly no longer in any mood to be tolerant. Please sit down." The sealing wax dripped softly on to the folded letter, and then Camilla pressed her signet ring into it. The ring bore Harry's crest, and she glanced instinctively toward his portrait.

Sophie sniffed and tried to collect herself before doing as she was told. She took a seat opposite Camilla, and started to fiddle with the dragon carving on the arm of her chair. "What will Lord Ennismount do, Lady Camilla?"

"I really don't know."

"He's going to tell the grand duchess and William's father, I know he is!" Sophie hid her face in her hands and began to cry.

"He'll be quite justified if he does," Camilla replied frankly. "Oh, don't look at me like that, for it's the truth. By continuing to meet after promising not to on the night of the ball, you and William have been proved to be totally untrustworthy and irresponsible."

Sophie avoided her eyes. "We only met tonight. It was the first time, I swear it."

"Don't lie, Sophie."

"I'm not!"

"Yes, you are. You and William met in the kitchens at Cavendish Square, and you'd arranged to meet again at the Cross Keys in Wantage, as well as by the south lodge bridge here, so tonight certainly wasn't the first time."

Sophie sat forward with a gasp. "How did you know—? Mary! She told you! I knew she was being sly with me!"

"Don't blame Mary, for you put her in an impossible position. She would have held her tongue about everything if Lord Ennismount hadn't put two and two together and realized she was your agent. What was she supposed to do when I confronted her? Cast all caution to the wind and not only risk her own livelihood but also that of her family, who depend upon Summerton Park? It was very reprehensible and selfish of you to involve her as you did, Sophie, so if anyone should bear the blame for all this, it's you. And William, of course."

Sophie's eyes flashed mutinously, but then she hesitated and nodded contritely. "You are right, Lady Camilla," she admitted.

"I know I am."

"But I do love William so." Sophie got up, and all pretense fell away at last as she went to the fireplace and stood looking down into the flames. "It—it is very difficult to be the czar's ward and know I must always do exactly what he wishes. He does not know me now because I have been away from Russia so long. It suits him to please the Grand Duchess Catherine by making me marry Prince Ludwig. He does not care if I am to be happy or not."

After Dominic's slip of the tongue by the pagoda, Camilla now had no doubt that Sophie was the czar's secret daughter, although it was equally clear that Sophie herself did not know it. If Sophie Arenburg was really Sophie Romanov, could the czar really be so hard as to brush her feelings aside so completely?

Sophie had no doubts. "The grand duchess is the most important person in the world to him, and he always does what she wishes. This marriage is a whim to her, and therefore to him, but it will affect me for the rest of my life. I know I have been foolish and willful, Lady Camilla, and I am very sorry for the trouble I've caused, but it is very difficult for me when I know William is the only man I will ever truly love and I cannot marry him. You may say I am too young, that at only seventeen I cannot possibly know my own heart, but I do. I met him on almost my first day in London, before I knew I was to marry Prince Ludwig, and I loved William at first sight. It was at an assembly at the Russian Embassy in Harley Street. He came into the room, we looked at each other, and we both knew. Not a word was said, we simply knew. Do you understand, Lady Camilla?"

The speech had been quietly uttered from the heart

and Camilla found it very affecting. There was nothing false or dramatized, just a simple and honest statement of fact. This was the real Sophie Arenburg, without the histrionics and affectations that usually surrounded her, and it was a Sophie to whom Camilla could warm far more.

Camilla got up and went to her. "I do understand, Sophie, and I believe you are truly and deeply in love with William."

Sophie was anxious. "You are not just saying that? you don't really think I am a silly little girl who will love someone else next week?"

"I'm not just saying it, I really believe you, Sophie."

With a glad cry Sophie flung her arms around her neck and burst into tears again. Camilla held her close and stroked her golden hair, and after a while Sophie drew back and wiped her eyes. "I could be so very happy with William, my whole life would be happy, but I must leave him, leave England, and be unhappy until the day I die."

"You may not be as unhappy with the prince as you think," Camilla offered encouragingly.

"Have you met him?"

"Prince Ludwig? No."

"He is very handsome, but he is also vain, spiteful, and heartless. He hurt many ladies in St. Petersburg and was unkind to me because I was only thirteen at the time. I shall be wretched if I am his wife, for he does not know how to give happiness. William knows how. When I am with him, I am in paradise." Sophie smiled sheepishly. "That is a silly thing to say, *non*? But it is how I feel."

"Sophie, you've just explained everything to me so

sincerely that I'm sure the czar will listen to you if you plead with him personally."

"He only listens to his favorite sister. The grand duchess can twist him around her little finger."

"Possibly, but the czar is coming here to a hero's welcome. There is peace after many years of war, and he will be lauded. That will surely put him in an excellent mood."

"He will still wish to please the grand duchess, and anyway there will be King Frederick of Prussia to consider. *He* will be here as well," Sophie reminded her.

Camilla didn't know what to say.

Sophie sighed. "I must also think of William. If I am truly very good from now on, maybe Lord Ennismount will not tell William's father about all this. I do not want William to be ruined because of me, Lady Camilla, in fact I could not bear it if that happened. I do not really have all the bravado I seem to." More tears welled from her eyes.

Camilla's heart went out to her. "Oh, Sophie, you must not think the worst. Lord Ennismount's temper might have cooled by the morning."

"But it may not. What will happen then?"

"I—I don't know."

"Will you speak to him for me?"

"Oh, I don't know . . ."

"Please, Lady Camilla! I know he will listen to you."

"Sophie, you're crediting me with more influence than I have. I will speak to him for you, but I can't promise I'll be successful."

Sophie hugged her. "Thank you, Lady Camilla."

"Now I think you should go to bed and try to sleep. You've had a very difficult night and you don't want to look ragged when you see William, do you?"

"No, I don't." Sophie smiled again. "I know you will make Lord Ennismount relent, Lady Camilla," she said. "Lady Camilla, may I say something impertinent?"

Camilla smiled. "You don't usually bother to ask."

"I know, but I have mended my ways, so may I say it?"

Camilla nodded. "I suppose so."

"I think you are in love with Lord Ennismount," Sophie said bluntly.

Camilla drew back sharply, and was suddenly conscious of Harry's portrait. "Sophie, I—"

"And I think Lord Ennismount loves you too," Sophie interrupted.

Camilla regained her equilibrium. "That I doubt very much. Sophie, you really don't know anything about it, so please leave it at that."

"I—I have offended you?"

"No, of course not."

With a relieved smile, Sophie gathered her skirts and hurried out.

Camilla looked guiltily up at Harry's portrait, and then turned away. It wasn't love that she felt for Dominic, it wasn't—

The sound of hooves came from outside and she glanced curiously toward the window. Who could be coming to the house at this hour? It wasn't even dawn yet. She went to hold a curtain aside. A horseman rode swiftly along the drive, and passed from sight as he approached the main entrance. A moment later she heard him at the door.

She left the drawing room and saw Hawkins going downstairs ahead of her, grumbling as he went. He had his coat on over his nightshirt, and was carrying a smoking candle which almost extinguished as he crossed the hall to open the door. She heard voices, and then the butler came back in and closed the door. The horseman rode away again.

"Who was it, Hawkins?" she called down.

"A messenger from London, my lady, with a very important communication for Lord Ennismount." The butler held up a sealed letter.

"Then take it directly to his lordship," she instructed.

Dominic suddenly spoke behind her. "There's no need, for I'm here," he said, going down the stairs to take the letter.

Hawkins withdrew again, and she watched as Dominic scanned the sheet of paper. When he'd finished he pressed his lips thoughtfully together and pushed the letter into his pocket.

"Is it bad news?"

"It is for Sophie." He retraced his steps to where she stood. "The grand duchess and Prince Ludwig are in London, and the former has made it crystal clear that not only is Sophie to be betrothed to the prince as soon as possible, but also that the wedding itself is to take place when the czar and King Frederick of Prussia arrive in June."

Camilla stared at him in astonishment. "The *wedding*?"

"I fear so, and before you ask if there's a chance I've been misinformed, let me say that the messenger came directly from Carlton House. At the moment the grand duchess thinks Sophie is recovering from influenza, but that excuse can only be dragged out for so long. Sophie will soon have to be declared well again, and then she must go to the grand duchess to prepare for an imminent London betrothal."

"It will break her heart."

"There's nothing we can do about that. The Prince Regent is most concerned that the grand duchess shall never hear about this de Marne affair, and to make certain a discreet veil is pulled over the whole business he has issued a warning that if Sophie carries out her threats to cause trouble in high places, he'll not only see that her character comes in for some very unwelcome scrutiny, but also that the Earl of Highnam is denied his lofty new title because of his son's scandalous behavior. This will result in William's ruin." Dominic exhaled slowly. "In short, the prince has implemented most of the threats I used by the pagoda, except that where I merely rattled them with no intention of actually doing anything, His Royal Highness fully means to carry them out unless Sophie does as he wishes. I'm therefore instructed to see she is minutely aware of the consequences should she choose to be headstrong."

Camilla was dismayed for Sophie. "Oh, I'm sure she won't do anything. She's already afraid of the czar's reaction should she forfeit her good name, and she's certainly anxious about any aftermath for William. You, er, made the necessary impression when you spoke as you did by the pagoda."

"I hope you're right, but it should be remembered that Sophie Arenburg has promised good conduct before."

"I know." Camilla looked at him. "Dominic, you refused to answer this before, but perhaps you will now. *Is* Sophie the czar's daughter?"

He hesitated, and then nodded. "But she doesn't know it," he said quickly.

"I realize that."

"Her mother was a Madame Arenburg, the beautiful wife of a Swedish diplomat in St. Petersburg. The late Monsieur Arenburg was prepared to accept paternity in exchange for a considerable sum of money, and on his and his wife's deaths, Sophie became the czar's 'ward.' The czar has bestowed a great fortune on her, which is why she's so attractive a proposition for Prince Ludwig. Czar Alexander is officially childless, which is why he has taken such a keen interest in Sophie. The Grand Duchess Catherine has persuaded him that it would be inappropriate for his only daughter to make anything other than a royal marriage."

"Poor Sophie," Camilla murmured, and then looked at him again. "Can I assume you don't intend to add to the difficulty with the Prince Regent?"

"Add to it? In what way?"

"Oh, come on, Dominic, the prince is only likely to find out about Sophie and William's disobedience if you tell him."

"What do you take me for? Damn it, Camilla, it's one thing to issue threats in order to achieve a modicum of good conduct, quite another to carry those threats out. I admit I'm angry with them both, but I don't intend to throw them to the lions, if only because I don't want to go down in history as one of the fools who couldn't control the latter-day Romeo and Juliet whose affair led to an international quarrel between Britain, Russia, and probably Prussia as well!"

"This latter-day Romeo and Juliet as you call them, are every bit as much in love as the originals," Camilla replied.

"Possibly, but they should remember their obligations, and as soon as de Marne's ankle permits, he's to leave this house, because it's far too risky to let him stay."

"How hard and unfeeling you sound."

"If it's hard and unfeeling to utter the truth——"

"What right do you have to adopt the moral high ground and condemn Sophie and William?" Camilla interrupted quietly. "If it's simply a matter of remembering obligations, perhaps you should have thought of that before you attempted to seduce your best friend's wife. I knew I was doing wrong and I've felt guilty ever since, but you, it seems, must have a clear conscience. How very agreeable it must be to feel so free to select one's principles."

"Convenient? Selecting one's principles is sometimes the hardest thing in the world, for whichever way one decides, morality is left by the wayside!" he replied.

"How profound, to be sure," she murmured, glancing away.

He put his hand to her cheek and made her look at him. "It's better you don't understand me, Camilla. I wish it were not so, but it is." His hand dropped away again. "As for having to tell Sophie and de Marne what lies ahead, I think we must tread with care. Don't say anything to them yet about the message from Carlton House. We must choose our time and words with infinite care. Sophie may seem to have seen the error of her ways, but we still don't want to run the risk of any, er, precipitate actions, such as an elopement, for instance." He hesitated. "Have you written to Elizabeth Oxforth?" he asked suddenly.

"Yes."

"I trust you've shown discretion?"

"If you're wondering if I've poured out every detail of our embarrassing inability to keep things under control, you may rest assured I haven't. I merely asked her to come because William was here with a broken ankle. I hope she responds swiftly, for she can take him back to London with her."

He gave a coldly wry smile. "Oh, you may rely upon it that she'll come; indeed, I was quite surprised when she didn't accompany us in the first place."

"Why do you say that?" Camilla asked, remembering how anxious Elizabeth had been to do just that.

"Oh, call it a hunch."

"You've been dabbling in politics for too long, Dominic, and now can't help talking in riddles," she said.

"I daresay," he murmured, turning to walk on to the apartment.

Camilla caught his arm. "You do promise we'll be lenient with Sophie and William when we tell them the news from London, don't you? I know you have every right to be angry with them, but when they learn there is no hope and Sophie's marriage is to take place in June, their hearts will be broken once and for all."

"I've already said we'll choose the time and words with care."

"I know, but—"

"Camilla, do you honestly think I'm not aware of how desperately heartbroken they're going to be? I assure you that if there's one thing I know about, it's heartbreak." He looked down into her anxious eyes. "Have you any idea at all how heartbroken *I* was when you married Harry? Do you know how *my* heart broke when you chose to stay with him after those stolen moments in the pagoda? No, I don't think you do, but it's water under the bridge now, and perhaps that's just as well, for you and I would clearly have done very badly together."

She stared after him as he went into his apartment and closed the door.

Chapter 17

Sophie and William had still to be told about the grand duchess's new plans when Elizabeth came post haste from London in response to Camilla's letter. It was nightfall at the end of a wet and windy day as she stepped down from her carriage.

Camilla hurried out to greet her. "Elizabeth! Oh, I'm so glad you came so quickly!"

"Of course I came quickly, for I mean to give that Arenburg creature a piece of my mind!" Elizabeth replied, shaking out her peach merino skirts.

Camilla was dismayed. "They're both at fault; you can't just blame Sophie," she said, shivering a little as the blustering wind fluttered her blue velvet skirts and blew a wisp of dark hair across her face.

"William would *never* have done this if it weren't for her!" Elizabeth replied sharply.

"You're being unreasonable."

"Oh, Camilla, how do you expect me to feel? I wanted to come here with you because I felt so uneasy about it all, and now I can't help thinking that if you'd agreed this might not have happened."

Camilla was nettled. "Are you suggesting Dominic and I have been negligent?"

"No, of course not," Elizabeth replied hastily. "Forgive me, I—I'm just not thinking clearly. When your letter arrived it reminded me of the last dreadful time you wrote to me like that. It brought everything back so much that I cried for over an hour."

"The last time . . . ? Oh, yes." Camilla looked away, for that other occasion had been when Harry died.

Elizabeth squeezed her arm. "Well, dire as the present situation is, it's not half so bad as then. Lord, it's cold out here. Can we go in? I'm afraid I have some more exceedingly disagreeable news to impart."

With a sinking heart, Camilla linked her arm and they went toward the house, but as they reached the steps something made Elizabeth glance back at the dark skies.

Her breath caught, and she halted. "Oh, wasn't that . . . ?"

Camilla paused as well. "What have you seen?"

"I'm sure I saw lightning."

"You must be mistaken. Apart from anything else, it's the wrong weather and wrong time of year." Camilla glanced up at the lowering clouds. Lightning? She prayed not, for thunderstorms were always a distressing reminder of Harry's death.

Elizabeth nodded. "You're right, of course. It's just . . ."

"Yes?"

"Well, thunder, this house, two years ago . . ."

"Please let's change the subject." Camilla quickly took her arm and ushered her into the brightly lit house, where Elizabeth immediately paused to look fondly around the lavish entrance hall.

"Every time I come here I'm taken back anew by

how astonishing a place this is. I vow there cannot be anything left in the Orient!"

"You said you had some more disagreeable news," Camilla prompted.

"Yes. It seems the Grand Duchess Catherine is impatient to see the Prussian match concluded as quickly as possible. She expects Mlle Arenburg to return to London as soon as she has recovered from her, er, 'influenza,' and then the actual wedding ceremony is to take place in—"

"In London in June," Camilla finished for her. "Yes, we already know."

"You do? Oh." Elizabeth was nonplussed. "I thought it would come as a shock to you out here in the sticks."

"Gloucestershire isn't quite the sticks," Camilla murmured.

Elizabeth went on. "You see, George was at Carlton House when Prinny first heard of the grand duchess's decision. He immediately came home and told me, so you can imagine how I felt when I received your note saying William was here! There's so much at stake, from Father's marquessate to George's friendship with Prinny. Heaven knows how badly this might reflect upon the latter, for the prince is clearly furious about the whole wretched business." Elizabeth unpinned her hat and put it down on a table. Then she looked a little reproachfully at Camilla. "To be frank, I feel you and Dominic could have shown more sense than to allow William to stay here."

Camilla was provoked. "Would you have preferred us to throw him out, injured ankle and all?"

"You could at least have seen him safely installed at

an inn, well away from that wretched Russian hoyden!" Elizabeth replied vehemently.

"So this is all *our* fault, is it? Your brother is the innocent victim of unfair circumstance? If that is your contention, Elizabeth, I think the sooner you leave, the better."

The firm rebuke found its mark. Elizabeth flushed and lowered her glance guiltily. "Of course William's at fault. I—I'm sorry, Camilla, I didn't mean to point a finger at you, it's just that I'm all of a dither about everything. Please take no notice."

"It's difficult to take no notice when you're so free with your accusations," Camilla replied a little coolly.

"Can't we forget I spoke?" Elizabeth pleaded. "Oh, don't let's quarrel, Camilla, we've been friends far too long to fall out over this."

Camilla managed a smile of sorts. "Yes, we have, haven't we?"

Elizabeth cast around for something to say. "Er, how did William hurt his ankle? Your note didn't say much."

"He fell from the staircase in the pagoda. He shouldn't have been able to get in because repairs are needed, but he'd arranged an assignation with Sophie."

"No doubt she plagued him into it," Elizabeth observed acidly.

"William doesn't need plaguing where Sophie's concerned," Camilla pointed out.

"She takes advantage of his soft heart."

"Oh, do stop this, Elizabeth. No one held a pistol to William's head and forced him to embark upon this affair, he did it of his own volition, and now we're all in a scrape because of it."

Elizabeth looked contrite again. "I'm being foolish, and you're right to tell me off."

"You're not being foolish, you're being downright infuriating," Camilla replied.

Something struck Elizabeth then. "How do you know about the grand duchess's new plans regarding the wedding? George told me almost as soon as Prinny learned."

"The prince sent word."

Elizabeth was shaken. "The prince?" she repeated.

"Yes, and perhaps I should tell you he not only informed us of the new urgency in the wedding plans, but also gave due warning that if word gets out about Sophie's indiscretions, or if Sophie carries out her threats, it will be the worst for her and for William."

Elizabeth went pale. "William? In—in what way?"

"Your father will be denied his elevation to marquess, and that will inevitably result in—"

"In William's disinheritance," Elizabeth finished for her. "Oh, Camilla, I had no idea that the prince had already taken action. He didn't tell George, which can only mean George's friendship is to be dispensed with as surely as Brummell's was last year. Oh, this is terrible!" She hid her face in her hands.

Camilla tried to comfort her. "You can't possibly read all that into it."

"Oh, yes, I can. Prinny has made it crystal clear that if any hint of this scandal rubs off on him . . ." Elizabeth couldn't finish the sentence.

"It won't rub off, Elizabeth, for we're all determined to keep the whole business under control. Everyone, including Sophie, is anxious for it to remain a secret, and that's how it will be, provided we all keep our heads."

"I can't imagine Mlle Arenburg will wish to oblige us!" Elizabeth declared savagely.

"She's afraid for William. You see, Elizabeth, contrary to your belief, she's deeply and sincerely in love with him, and she's already begun to accept that she can't prevent the inevitable. Dominic and I have been waiting for the right moment to tell William and her what the Prince Regent's message contained."

Elizabeth studied her. "How cozy you both sound, to be sure. Almost like an old married couple."

Dominic's voice entered the proceedings. "I'm surprised you equate marriage with coziness, Lady Elizabeth," he said, descending the staircase after eavesdropping on everything they'd said.

A dull flush stained Elizabeth's cheeks. "Good evening, sir," she said stiffly.

"Good evening. My, how very speedily you've arrived. I vow your carriage wheels must have struck sparks along the highway."

She gave him a stony look. "You surely didn't imagine I'd take my time?"

He gave a short laugh as he reached them. "You? My dear lady, I'd be the first to confirm that you are usually astonishingly prompt."

"You don't improve with the years, sir."

"Nor do you," he replied cordially. "Words fail me that you should attempt to absolve your brother of any blame. Only a milksop would be incapable of standing up to a young woman barely out of the schoolroom, but apparently you are content to fix him with that paltry label. As for blaming Camilla and me for his presence here, let me assure you we're only too conscious of the awkwardness of the situation, so conscious we wish you to remove him as soon as you possibly can."

"I've already apologized for being so foolishly biased in my brother's favor, but even you must admit that Mlle Arenburg is willful to a fault."

"No one denies it, madam, but she's only seventeen, whereas William has not only reached his majority, but is also betrothed to Alice Penshill *and* has already been castigated for commencing this exceedingly ill-judged liaison. His conduct is indefensible, and I don't expect any delay before you relieve us of his irksome presence. It wouldn't do for Prinny to find out where he is, would it?"

"I intend to take him away as soon as possible, sir," Elizabeth replied coldly.

"Good." Dominic's eyes shone as he held her gaze, and then his lips curved into a disdainful smile. "I'm sure you'd like to pretend William is your sole reason for coming here, but he's only part of it, isn't he? What a horror you must have of all those old ashes being raked over again."

"Old ashes? I don't know what you mean."

"My, how the boards must weep for never having known your tread," he murmured. "However, my prime concern at the moment is how and when Sophie and William are informed about developments, and until Camilla and I have decided exactly how to go about it, I forbid you to say anything to either of them. You may tell your brother you're here because of his broken ankle, but no mention is to be made of the wedding plans being brought forward. Is that clear?"

"By what right do you presume to order me?" Elizabeth said furiously.

"By right of being here on the instructions of both

the Prince Regent and the prime minister, whereas you are only here to safeguard your own selfish interests."

Elizabeth's voice shook with anger as she replied. "I'm here because Camilla asked me."

He gave a thin smile. "As I've already said, William is only part of it. You'd have come here soon anyway, because you can't bear it that I'm in this house."

"I despise you," she breathed.

His smile didn't falter. "Good, for I'd hate to have your so-called friendship."

Camilla felt very uncomfortable. "Please stop this. I know the situation is awkward for all of us, but we'll achieve nothing if all we do is trade insults. We aren't the only people concerned in this, Sophie and William are very much involved, and we can't put off telling them for much longer."

Dominic nodded. "I don't relish the prospect."

"Nor do I."

Elizabeth shrugged. "Then let me do it. I see no purpose in delaying."

Dominic shook his head swiftly. "It must be left to Camilla and me, for I have no doubt how tender an intervention yours would be, especially for Sophie."

"William's my brother, and I'm the one who should tell him," Elizabeth insisted.

Camilla sighed. "No, Elizabeth. Dominic's right, he and I should be the ones to break the tidings. We'll do it after dinner tonight, when everyone has calmed down a little."

But Elizabeth was impatient to have it over and done with. "Why wait?"

Camilla looked at her. "Because Sophie has a

headache and is lying down. She's been dreadfully upset by all this and needs to rest. I certainly don't intend to disturb her in order to break such disagreeable tidings."

Elizabeth shrugged. "Oh, very well. I just feel that the sooner they're told, the sooner William and I can leave."

"Dinner will be in about an hour and a half. I'm sure Dominic and I will have decided what to say by then."

"Would that I could feel as optimistic, but I won't do anything to rock matters, you have my word on it."

At that moment a distant roll of thunder echoed through the gathering darkness outside. It was accompanied by a spattering of rain against the windows, and in the space of a heartbeat they were all painfully reminded of the past.

It was as if Harry's wraith had joined them, and Camilla felt it so strongly she could almost see him. To break the sudden spell, she turned swiftly to Hawkins, who waited at a discreet distance to escort Elizabeth to the room that had been prepared for her arrival. "Hawkins, attend to her ladyship, if you please."

"Madam. Please come this way, my lady," he said to Elizabeth, who inclined her head and went with him.

The thunder rolled again, and Dominic spoke softly. "The past isn't what it seems, Camilla."

"No? Then what is it?" she challenged.

He hesitated, wanting to tell her all he knew, but again he stepped back from the brink. "It doesn't matter."

"The past doesn't matter? You're wrong, sir, for the past matters very much where you and I are concerned." Gathering her skirts, she walked away, and as she did she felt as if she brushed past Harry.

Chapter 18

Elizabeth changed out of her traveling clothes into a fuchsia pink gown that was suitable for dinner, and then went to see William. She intended to stand by the agreement as to how and when he and Sophie should learn of the developments that would affect them so, but that wasn't how it turned out.

William's room was candlelit, for it was now completely dark outside. He was sitting by the fire, with his injured leg propped on a little stool. Another growl of thunder stole across the heavens beyond the tightly drawn curtains, and the wind drew the chimney, making the fire glow. He sat forward in surprise as his sister walked in unannounced.

"Elizabeth!"

"I'm sure you're delighted to see me, brother mine," she said, closing the door.

"I knew Camilla had written to you, but I didn't expect you to come quite so swiftly."

"I was ever the concerned and loving sibling," she murmured, leaning back against the door and studying him in the candlelight. "How could you do this, William?"

"Because I'm in love with Sophie."

"Really? How sweet. Don't let it bother you that George might forfeit his close friendship with the Prince Regent, that Father might be denied his marquessate, or that you happen to be betrothed to Alice Penshill. And heaven forfend that it should even cross your mind to remember dear Sophie's imminent betrothal to royalty. No, don't let that be of any concern, for all you must do is think of yourself!"

"Follow your example, you mean?" he retorted defensively.

She left the door and came to stand by the fire. "I admit to many a selfish sin, William, but I've never done anything that would harm my family."

"Your halo is positively blinding," he muttered, shifting his sore foot and wincing.

"Your facetious quips don't impress me when I've just suffered the insult of being ordered to remove you from this house."

"I didn't expect to be allowed to stay."

"No? You surprise me, for your conduct has been so arrogantly thoughtless of late that it's quite conceivable you might think you should be allowed to do as you please." Suddenly she changed the subject. "How are Camilla and Dominic getting on?"

"Eh? What's that got to do with it?"

"Just answer me."

William shrugged. "I don't really know how they're getting on. To be truthful, I haven't been taking much notice."

"Nevertheless, you must have some idea," she pressed. "How do they behave toward each other?"

"There are definite undercurrents."

"What sort of undercurrents?"

"About Harry, I suppose. Sometimes it's so bad one can almost slice the atmosphere with a knife."

"So they aren't becoming close again?"

"I don't think so."

"I need to know, William. It's important."

He frowned. "What is this? I've told you what I think, and can't say more. I don't know what they say and do when I'm not there, nor do I particularly care. I've got problems of my own, in case you've forgotten."

"Forgotten? I'd dearly like to enjoy that privilege, William, but your actions have made it quite impossible! I don't think you have any conception of how disastrous this could be for the family. We might even be excluded from court circles! This isn't some mild provincial stir, it's a stir on a grand scale, and all because you and dear little Sophie want to have your own way. It isn't always possible to have what one wants, William, and the sooner you realize that sad fact, the better!"

He avoided her eyes by looking steadfastly into the fire. Rain dashed against the window as more thunder rolled over the park, and Elizabeth glanced toward the sound. "It was like this when Harry died," she murmured.

William didn't respond. He and Sophie were about to be driven apart forever, so what did it matter if there had been thunder on the day Sir Harry Summerton went to his Maker?

The silence was broken by a soft tapping at the door and Sophie's low voice. "William? Can I come in?"

He glanced uneasily at his sister, for Sophie couldn't have chosen a worse moment. Elizabeth's face was set as she crossed the room and flung the door open. "Do come in, Mademoiselle Arenburg!"

The diamonds in Sophie's hair flashed in the candlelight as she gasped and stepped back. "Lady Elizabeth!"

"The same. Come inside, mademoiselle, for there are things I wish to say to you!"

Sophie obeyed reluctantly, edging past Elizabeth and then hurrying across to William in a rustle of silver taffeta. He caught her hands as she knelt beside him. "It's all right, my dearest . . ." he murmured, drawing her palm to his lips.

Elizabeth closed the door sharply. "How touching," she said acidly. "William says it's all right, and, hey presto, it is. Except that it isn't, indeed it's all the very opposite."

Sophie's lilac eyes crept anxiously to him. "What is she saying?"

"That she's been sent for to take me away from here."

"But—"

"It's for the best. Your reputation . . ."

Elizabeth's anger bubbled over. "*Her* reputation! What about everyone else? Oh, I'm really tired of this. Why should others have to suffer because Sophie Arenburg is a spoiled, self-indulgent, mischievous, and downright exasperating chit?"

"Elizabeth!" William cried, struggling to his feet, but pain jabbed through his ankle and he fell back again with a gasp.

Elizabeth felt no remorse. Sophie, the root of all the trouble, was suddenly at her mercy, and all promises to Camilla and Dominic were forgotten as she gave in to the urge to vent her spleen. "I wish you'd stayed in

Russia, miss, for your pampered and tiresome ways are surely more suited to St. Petersburg than anything here in England. You don't deserve a royal match, but that's precisely what you're going to have. The Grand Duchess Catherine expects you to return to London as soon as possible, because you're going to marry Prince Ludwig in June, when the czar and the Emperor Frederick arrive!"

Sophie's face went white. "No . . ."

"Oh, yes. So you see, my dear mademoiselle, your little diversion with my fool of a brother is at an end. You and he are never going to be together, and it won't be long before you're far away in some dark corner of Prussia, where I trust you'll rot!"

Sophie rose slowly to her feet. She was trembling from head to toe and her eyes were wide with dismay. "I will not marry Prince Ludwig! I will *not*!"

"You have no choice."

Sophie began to sob. "I—I'll tell the grand duchess that the Prince Regent and the British government have been trying to turn me from this match! I'll—"

"Do that and the prince will see my brother disinherited. You'll have that on your conscience for all time if you carry out your childish threats." Elizabeth was enjoying her revenge, and felt no conscience at all as she twisted the dagger in Sophie's wounds.

William stared at his sister in disbelief. "Elizabeth, there's no need to—"

"There's every need, otherwise this provoking little trollop won't pay heed to the unsavory truth."

His eyes hardened with fury. "Don't speak of Sophie like that!"

"I'll speak as I choose! I'm tired of your Mlle Arenburg, and I don't intend to put up with her nonsense any longer. She is putting our entire family into difficulty, and I see no reason whatsoever why we should endure it without hitting back!"

William held his sister's gaze. "If anyone has put the family at risk, it's me," he said quietly.

"You wouldn't have done any of this without encouragement from her," Elizabeth answered.

Sophie was distraught. "Please, Lady Elizabeth, do not say such terrible things, for I love William with all my heart," she whispered.

"It's my brother today, my dear, but who will it be next week? I doubt if you're capable of constancy. I look at you and see my own reflection. I know you for what you are, a fickle, self-centered hussy, with thoughts only for yourself. Just as I was at your age."

"It's not true!" Sophie cried wretchedly, her cheeks wet with tears.

"Every word is true, and you know it," Elizabeth replied coldly.

William struggled up from the chair, his eyes dark with anger as he faced his sister. "I'll never forgive you for this, Elizabeth," he breathed.

"The prospect leaves me cold," she replied. A fury had been unleashed inside her, and the need to hurt came pouring out in a vitriolic torrent. "Your precious little Arenburg is going to marry Prince Ludwig, and after all the trouble she's caused me and mine, I pray he won't make her happy."

"I don't think I know you anymore, Elizabeth."

"I don't care about your little mademoiselle, William, because if it were not for her, Camilla and Dominic would not be—" Elizabeth broke off, her lips closing abruptly.

William searched her face. "Well, go on, you might

as well finish it. If it were not for Sophie, Camilla and Dominic wouldn't what?"

"It doesn't matter."

"But it does, Elizabeth. You obviously have some deep reason for behaving like this, and I think Sophie and I deserve to be told what it is."

A nerve flickered at Elizabeth's temple and she turned away. "It's no concern of yours."

"I'm making it my concern! What have Camilla and Dominic got to do with all this?" William snapped.

Sophie was distracted. "Stop! Oh, please stop! What does it matter why Lady Elizabeth has said the things she has? All that matters is that we can't be together, William, and I cannot do anything about it because if I do I will hurt you. That is something I could never do, my love! And so I will marry Prince Ludwig and go hundreds of miles away from any hope of happiness."

"Oh, Sophie, my dearest darling . . ." William tried to pull her into his arms, but she pushed him away.

"No! I cannot bear it!" Tears were wet on her cheeks and she ran from the room as another rumble of thunder sounded outside.

William turned on his sister. "Get out of here, madam, for I never wish to see your face again. I'll leave Summerton Park, but not with you, of that you may be sure."

Sophie's tearful flight didn't bring Elizabeth the sense of triumph she'd anticipated, and the aversion in William's eyes washed over her like icy water. "William, I . . ."

"I have nothing more to say to you."

"Please listen to me."

"You've said more than enough; now get out of here."

Elizabeth lowered her eyes and without another word withdrew from the room.

William picked up the makeshift crutches with which he'd been provided, and then went after Sophie.

While the confrontation took place in William's room, Dominic was at the window in his own apartment, watching the progress of the storm along the valley.

The window overlooked the stable block, and the rain shone in the glow of the yard lanterns. Lightning flashed and thunder rumbled across the dark skies. Time stood still for a moment, and then began to roll backward. The stormy April night was left behind, and suddenly he was plunged back to the humid summer day that Sir Harry Summerton met his death.

He stared down into the past, watching himself riding back from watching Harry meet his mistress at the villa. The thunderstorm that had been threatening was now approaching fast, and could almost be smelled in the draft of wind that breathed across the stableyard.

Rain fell as he dismounted and handed the reins to a groom, then there was a clatter of hooves as the Tattersall's roan was led in from the paddock.

"Has Sir Harry requested the horse?" he asked, as lightning sliced the sky overhead.

The groom nodded. "Yes, my lord. Before he went out, he asked for it to be ready in an hour from now, though I don't know if he'll still want it in this weather. To my mind he's ill-advised to ride such a brute in any conditions, let alone thunder," the man added as the storm made the stallion toss its head and caper nervously about.

Dominic could only agree.

The storm had intensified an hour later as he returned to the stables to wait for Harry. The roan was saddled and waiting in the stall, but it moved restlessly to and fro each time there was a crack of thunder. He leaned on the stable door, watching the rain and thinking what a fool Harry was to risk his marriage for charms far too many others had sampled before him. Titled as she was, the lady was far from exclusive.

The rain fell relentlessly, and the air tingled with electricity before each resounding thunderclap. The stallion became more and more unnerved. Its neck was damp with sweat and it was clearly too overwrought to be ridden. At the best of times it was a mount that would require the control of a rider of steel: Harry Summerton was not such a rider.

At last Harry rode swiftly into the yard, and handed his horse to the groom who reluctantly ventured out to greet him. Dominic heard him shout above the racket of the storm.

"Keep the roan in readiness, I'll take it out the moment the weather improves."

"Yes, sir."

Then Harry tugged his top hat low over his forehead to run toward the house, but Dominic called him.

"Harry, I want a word!"

Startled, Harry hurried across to the stall, removing his hat and shaking the moisture from it as he looked at him. "What on earth are you doing here?"

"I've been waiting for you."

Harry searched his face. "Oh?"

"Yes, and I think you can guess what I'm going to say."

"I've no idea."

"I know why you've been in such a base humor these past weeks."

Harry smiled. "Do you, indeed?" he murmured.

"Yes, and you have her installed in a villa just beyond the park. You've come from her now."

Harry's smile faded. "Fouché would appear to be your middle name."

"It's got to stop, and Camilla must never know."

"Who in the hell do you think you are?" Harry demanded curtly.

"I'm someone who wishes to protect Camilla from ever discovering what a misbegotten louse you really are."

"You're free with your insults."

"You couldn't afford my compliments. Face facts, Harry, I mean to have this whole business satisfactorily sorted before Camilla returns from Tetbury." Dominic glanced at the stableyard clock. "She could return at any moment now, so I want your word you're about to become the perfect husband again."

"Your impudence astounds me, for what damned business is it of yours in the first place?" Harry replied angrily.

"I'm making it my business."

"Why? Because you've developed an itch for my wife?"

Dominic became still. "I'll forget you said that."

Harry gave a short laugh. "How noble, to be sure. Come on, Dominic, I know *exactly* how you feel about Camilla, and—"

"Don't say another word, for you have no conception at all how I feel toward her," Dominic breathed icily, for it was all he could do to contain his fury and distaste. He wondered if he'd ever really known Harry Summerton, for the man into whose eyes he looked now was a callous stranger.

Harry gave a thin smile. "My, my, how pure you'd like me to think you are, but I've seen the lust in your eyes when you look at Camilla. You're a hypocrite, Dominic, wanting my wife, while at the same time condemning me for wanting someone else's."

"I'm no saint, Harry, but there's a world of difference between what I feel for Camilla and what you're doing. I love her with all my heart, and I've done so since before your marriage. I thought you loved her as much as she loved you, so I didn't attempt to come between husband and wife, but then I discovered you were deceiving her with a woman who is little better than a whore. I admit I've now tried to steal Camilla from you, but she cannot be stolen."

"So this is nothing more or less than jealousy! You can't have what you want, so I can't have what I want either?" Harry was scathing.

"I'm merely protecting Camilla."

"Ha! Nobility again! Well, if you ask me Camilla doesn't want your protection, she wants your passion! I know my wife; your burning looks have made the desired impression, and she's ripe for seduction."

"Have a care how you speak of her!"

"Why, I do perceive that behind Fouché there lurks a veritable Sir Galahad," Harry murmured mockingly, his voice almost inaudible as another clash of thunder shook the sky.

"I don't give a damn about you, Harry, but I care very much about her."

"And if I tell you to go to hell?"

"I wouldn't advise it."

"How tedious you are, to be sure. Well, I'm not about to dance to your tune, Dominic, and as for Camilla, to be truthful I find her dull fare these days. Enjoy her if you wish, I'll even turn a blind eye if you get her between the sheets here. Just be discreet, old boy, I don't fancy having to act the outraged husband."

Dominic's disgusted fury spilled over, and he brought his clenched fist crashing up to Harry's jaw. Caught unawares, Harry staggered backward into the roan, making it whinny and rear.

A flash of lightning illuminated the gloom as Harry recovered and lunged back. The two men struggled, trading blow for blow, and the terrified stallion plunged from one side of the stall to the other.

Suddenly Harry flung himself sideways to snatch a rake from the wall. Grasping it in both hands, he swung it furiously at Dominic, who didn't quite manage to duck out of the way and was caught a glancing blow on the head. It was enough to daze him, and he fell dangerously close to the horse's flashing hooves.

He lay so still that Harry thought he was dead and dropped the rake just as an earsplitting thunderclap exploded directly overhead. The rain became a cloudburst as Harry stared numbly down at what he thought was Dominic's lifeless body. Then he was seized with panic. Snatching the roan's reins, he led it out into the storm. The horse reared and tried to break free, but somehow he managed to mount. Then he kicked his heels and urged the animal across the yard to the open park.

The clatter of hooves penetrated Dominic's daze,

and he struggled to his feet, still reeling from the fury of the blow. Realization swept sickeningly over him as he saw the open door, and he staggered out into the rainswept yard, calling Harry's name.

But Harry urged the horse on without hearing. Lightning turned the countryside white, and the earth shook as more thunder discharged above the park. The roan swerved violently to one side, and he was flung heavily to the ground. His head was dashed against a protruding tree root, killing him instantly, and at the very moment the breath left his body, Camilla's carriage drove in through the gates on its way back from Tetbury.

Dominic experienced it all again as he watched from the window, but then time turned once more and the daylit past faded into the darkness of the present. He stared down into the storm-drenched yard, where the lanterns swayed in the gusting wind. "I hope you're rotting in hell, Harry," he whispered as another roll of thunder echoed across the sky.

A slight figure in a hooded cloak hurried toward the stalls. The wind caught the hood and whipped it back. He stared at Sophie's tearstained face. She ran into the first stall, and the horse inside stirred nervously. It was Camilla's newly acquired roan, so like the one Harry had ridden . . .

Dominic put his hands on the sill and leaned urgently forward. What in God's name . . . ? As he watched, Sophie lifted a sidesaddle down from the shelf.

He needed no second bidding, but ran from the room.

was the cause of Dominic's presence here. Camilla,

Chapter 19

But as Dominic ran toward the staircase, he heard Camilla's alarmed voice from the hall below.

"William! For heaven's sake tell me what's wrong!"

"Let me go, Camilla! I must stop Sophie!" William cried.

Dominic reached the gallery and saw them at the foot of the stairs, which a distraught William had somehow managed to descend on his crutches. He was trying to go to the front door, but Camilla held his arm as she pleaded with him.

"You can't go out in this storm, William! *Please* tell me what's happened!"

In the split second before Dominic hurried down to them, he saw a motionless figure standing in the shadows to his right. It was Elizabeth. Her attention was on the scene on the stairs, and she didn't even glance toward him. She made no move to go to her brother's aid, indeed she seemed almost detached, as if everything was now out of her hands.

William tried to pull free of Camilla. "I must go to Sophie!" he insisted.

"What about Sophie?" she demanded as Dominic reached them.

"She's running away!" William cried desperately.

Camilla was aghast.

William turned to look bitterly at Elizabeth. "I despise you," he breathed, his voice carrying clearly in the moments before the storm echoed across the night again.

Elizabeth turned and walked away.

Neither Dominic nor Camilla needed to be told any more, for it was clear that Elizabeth had broken her word by telling Sophie everything as cruelly as possible.

Dominic put a reassuring hand on William's arm. "I'll go after Sophie. She went to the stables; I saw from my window."

William stared anxiously after him as he went out into the storm. Camilla waited only a moment before gathering her blue velvet skirts to hurry out as well. The rain was torrential, but she paid scant heed. Lightning transformed the night into dazzling day, and then darkness returned.

Dominic ran toward the roan's stall, calling out to Sophie as he went. But the past was with him again, and he heard that other day, when he'd shouted Harry's name into the fury of a storm.

Sophie had managed to saddle the frightened horse, although her hands shook so much she hadn't been able to tighten the girth properly. She was too distressed to be sensible, and was trying to mount as Dominic burst into the stall and caught the horse's bridle.

"Don't be foolish, Sophie!" he shouted.

"Leave me alone, *milord*!" she sobbed, trying to drag herself up to the saddle.

"No, damn it! I'm not having history repeat itself to the very last detail!" Seizing her around the waist, he pulled her roughly away from the horse. Then he slapped the animal's haunch and with a clatter of hooves it galloped out into the yard.

Camilla pressed back against a wall and closed her eyes weaky as it passed. This was all a bad dream . . . "Harry," she whispered, blinking back tears.

Sophie was hysterical. "You should not have done that, Lord Ennismount! You should have let me go. I don't want to stay now!"

"You can't go anywhere in this!" Dominic cried, pointing at the wild night.

"I wish I were dead!" Sophie wept, hiding her face in her hands.

"No, you don't," Dominic said more gently, putting his arms around her and holding her close.

"Lady Elizabeth said such terrible things . . ."

"Yes, I fear she probably did." His eyes met Camilla's as she came into the stall.

Sophie clung to him now. "Tell me it isn't true that I must be married to Prince Ludwig in June," she begged. "Tell me Lady Elizabeth only said it because she hates me."

He couldn't reply.

Camilla went to the weeping girl. "Let's go back inside, Sophie. Poor William is beside himself with worry over you," she said.

Sophie allowed herself to be led away, but Dominic spoke as they reached the door.

"Camilla?"

She turned.

His eyes were bright and intense. "I could stop it this time, but I swear there was nothing I could do before. You must believe me."

She gazed at him for a long moment, and then ushered Sophie out into the rain.

William was waiting anxiously in the entrance hall, and Sophie ran to him the moment she and Camilla came in. One of his crutches fell to the floor as he caught his love close, resting his cheek against her wet hair.

He glanced at Camilla. "Elizabeth was savage with her."

Camilla felt a little guilty. "Dominic and I were going to tell you both tonight, and Elizabeth promised she wouldn't say anything before then."

"My sister could hardly wait to break the news as poisonously as possible. It was as if seeing Sophie goaded her into it." He told her what Elizabeth had said.

Camilla lowered her eyes. What on earth had possessed Elizabeth? "I'm afraid she's a little, er, unreasonable about this whole thing," she said lamely.

"Unreasonable? She's positively vicious." He stroked Sophie's hair, and then looked at Camilla again. "She blames Sophie for more than just this affair with me."

"That can't be so."

"It is, Camilla. I don't know what it is, except that it's something to do with you and Dominic, and it's important enough to make her turn on Sophie."

She stared at him, but before anything more could be said Dominic spoke from the doorway behind them. "So dear Elizabeth couldn't hold her tongue," he said, taking off his wet coat and tossing it on to a marble-topped table.

His voice shook with barely controlled fury, and Camilla looked anxiously at him. "I—I'm sure she regrets it now. She simply lost her temper."

"Don't apologize for her, Camilla. She has no redeeming qualities, as I've always known but you've yet to comprehend. I want her out of this house tonight."

"Tonight? Oh, but—"

"Tonight, Camilla," he interrupted. "Send riders with her as far as the nearest inn if you're concerned for her safety, but see that she leaves here without delay." He didn't wait for her reply, but went up the staircase two steps at a time.

Camilla stared after him, and then looked at William. "Take Sophie into the library, William, it's always warm in there."

He nodded, and limpingly ushered his weeping beloved toward the library door.

Hawkins was waiting nearby and Camilla beckoned him. "See that a not drink is taken to them, Hawkins, and tell Mary she's to attend Mamselle directly."

"My lady."

Holding her damp velvet skirts, Camilla followed Dominic up the staircase, but long before she reached the top she heard angry voices coming from Elizabeth's room.

"I trust you're satisfied with your efforts, madam?" Dominic said coldly.

"It was no more than the little *chienne* deserved," Elizabeth replied.

"The little *chienne*, as you call her, is worth six of you."

"Sophie Arenburg needs taking in hand, sir, and as far as I can see you and Camilla have been singularly ineffectual so far."

"We don't need your advice, madam. My God, I marvel you have the gall to set foot in this house again, but I suppose I shouldn't really be surprised. You've always displayed an astonishing lack of principle, and this evening's exhibition is typical."

"I'd prefer it if you left this room, sir."

"Oh, I'm sure you would, but I haven't said my piece yet."

"You and I have nothing to say to each other," Elizabeth said stiffly, but an uneasy edge had crept into her voice.

"A great deal has been left unsaid for too long, madam. You've only escaped because I've held my tongue, but after tonight's episode I've had enough of you."

"I think not, for you have Camilla to consider," Elizabeth replied smoothly.

Camilla had been about to enter the room, but now drew back out of sight to listen.

Dominic spoke softly. "Yes, I have Camilla to consider, I've *always* considered her, and I always will, but perhaps the time has come to tell her the truth, the whole truth, and nothing but the truth."

"And destroy her? I think not."

"What an evil hag you are, to be sure," he breathed.

"Evil, no, but calculating, yes. I was afraid when I first heard you were accompanying Camilla here. Dear God, how I despise that little Russian hussy for the trouble she's caused, but now I feel safe again. You're not going to tell Camilla anything, you still love her too much, and that is my protection."

"Don't be so sure."

"You made your decision, no one made it for you."

"Harry made it for me when he died with his damned reputation intact!" Dominic snapped.

Outside, Camilla felt suddenly very, very cold, and it wasn't simply because of her damp clothes. What hadn't she been told? What did these two know that she didn't?

Elizabeth gave a clever laugh. "Yes, he did, didn't he? And what a predicament that left you in. Poor Dominic, forced into honorable silence to spare dear Camilla. But there's something I've always wondered—how did you find out?"

"It didn't take a genius. The pointers were there, and I followed him on the day he died. I saw him with you at that house. Dear God, it simply didn't occur to Camilla why you managed to arrive so swiftly when she sent for you. She thought you'd come from London, but you were barely two miles away all the time. You and Harry were despicable in every way, and certainly deserved each other."

Camilla's lips parted, and her heart stopped within her. Elizabeth and Harry?

Elizabeth laughed again. "Yes, we did, rather. He was certainly my most inventive lover, and I have no doubt I offered him more satisfaction than a goody-goody like Camilla."

"You're a whore, madam, with a whore's skills and a whore's heart. What would you know of a woman like Camilla? What would you know about winning a man's love and keeping it? Your looks are already on the wane, and what will happen to you then? How many lovers will continue to worship at the shrine? Precious few, of that you may be sure. George even finds a hand of cards more stimulating. As for your sons, I doubt they appreciate the reputation their mother has gained. But what does all that matter? I daresay your memories will be a comfort in your lonely old age."

"Get out this instant," Elizabeth hissed.

"No, madam, you get out. I want you from this house immediately."

"And are you the master here?" Elizabeth challenged, but then her breath caught as Camilla appeared in the doorway. "Camilla!"

Dominic whirled about in dismay.

Camilla was cold and shaking. What she'd heard had torn her world apart. She wished it was a dream, but she was only too wide awake. She held Elizabeth's gaze. "Dominic isn't the master here, Elizabeth, but I'm certainly the mistress, and I want you to leave right now."

"Camilla, I—"

"Don't say anything, for every word you've ever uttered to me has been a lie. You've never been my friend, and I wish to God I'd never met you." Camilla's face was ashen with shock.

Elizabeth hurried across to her. "Please listen to me. You misheard what I said."

"I heard everything only too clearly. Harry was your lover, and for that I will never forgive you. Or him. Now please leave this house immediately, before I have you forcibly thrown out." Without waiting for Elizabeth to say anything more, Camilla turned on her heel and walked away.

Dominic came after her and caught her arm. "Camilla, you must let me explain!"

"Let me go, for I despise you for keeping the truth from me!"

"I tried to protect you!" he cried, still holding her arm.

She wrenched herself free and struck him furiously across the face. "You knew! All the time you knew, and you said nothing! What a fool you made of me, letting me believe Harry loved me when all the time he and Elizabeth were . . ." She could not finish, but gathered her skirts to flee tearfully to the sanctuary of her apartment.

Chapter 20

It had stopped raining just before midnight when Elizabeth left Summerton Park.

Her carriage drove smartly away from the house, its lamps swinging through the darkness as the coachman brought the team up to a smart trot. Two armed men rode behind to see she didn't fall prey to a highwayman before reaching the nearest inn. Only extenuating circumstances would lead to a female guest being ejected at such an hour, but no one could deny Camilla was more than justified in ordering her late husband's mistress off her land.

No one said good-bye. Camilla remained in her apartment, and William curtly declined his sister's tentatively offered olive branch. It would be a very long time indeed before he forgave her for speaking to Sophie as she had.

Dominic was the only one who saw the carriage drive away from the steps. He watched the lamps fade away into the darkness, and then glanced up at the night sky. The storm had moved to the east now, with only an occasional distant growl to mark its progress. The air was fresh and cold, an owl hooted in the woods, and stars could be seen here and there as the clouds began to break up.

What a day this had been, he thought. The truth was finally out in the open, and he felt drained of emotion. He'd striven for so long to protect Camilla from Harry's affair with Elizabeth that he could hardly believe the lies were at an end. But although the pretense was over, his punishment would go on. The anguish and accusation in Camilla's eyes had stabbed him like a dagger. She felt betrayed by his silence, and maybe she was right to feel that way. He'd made a decision to shield her on the day Harry died, but who was to say it was the right decision? Camilla certainly didn't think it was. Oh, God, what a mess . . .

Taking a deep breath, he turned to go into the house. For a moment he considered trying to speak to her again, but then thought better of it. He was probably the last person she wanted to see. Besides, he had other obligations. He glanced toward the library. William and Sophie had the right to know everything, and William was certainly due an explanation for his sister's conduct.

The young lovers were locked in an embrace, and pulled guiltily apart as he entered. They expected him to be angry, but he merely smiled a little as he closed the door. "Gather ye rosebuds while ye may, *mes enfants*," he murmured. "Besides, I'm past outrage for the time being."

William looked closely at him. "Are you going to tell us what all this is really about?"

"I am. It started before Harry Summerton's death, and I'm ashamed to say I've allowed it to color my judgment where you're concerned, William. You see, I found it impossible to regard you as a person in your own right, to me you were Lady Elizabeth Oxforth's brother, and as such to be condemned out of hand. I trust you won't blame me too much when you know why." He went to pour himself a large glass of cognac. "Please sit down, for it's a long story, and I doubt if you're going to enjoy hearing it."

William sat down awkwardly, stretching his sore leg out before him. Sophie was about to take a chair opposite but then changed her mind and sat on the floor beside him, her head resting against his knee.

Dominic took up a position by the fireplace, leaning a hand on the mantel and gazing into the fire for a long moment before speaking. "It really began before Harry and Camilla were married, because that's when I first fell in love with her. She wasn't indifferent to me by any means, but she remained true to her promises to Harry. She became his wife, but part of her has always been mine, even though she would be the first to deny it."

William and Sophie sat in silence as he related the tangled tale, although their silence turned to shock when they learned of Elizabeth's affair with Harry.

William sat forward in dismay. "My sister and Harry Summerton?"

"Yes. It was a sufficiently passionate liaison for them to risk her being installed in a house near here so they could continue to meet. He was completely taken up with her, and was short-tempered and disagreeable toward Camilla." Dominic glanced at William. "Pure ill chance caused you to arrange to meet Sophie close to that same house. You can see it from the bridge by the south lodge. It didn't help your cause with me, as you may imagine."

William exhaled slowly. "Yes, I can understand that. Anyway, go on. What happened?"

"It wasn't until I followed Harry there and saw him with your sister that I actually knew for certain she was the one. I'd guessed he had a mistress, and I suspected it might be Elizabeth, but I couldn't be sure. I wasn't without sin at the time, for I tried to take Camilla from him, but she chose him, and I loved her too much to do anything but honor her decision. But I was determined to see he did the right thing by her." Quietly he told them of the confrontation that led to Harry's death.

Sophie's eyes widened and she put her hands to her mouth. William stared at him. "Harry thought you were dead?"

Dominic nodded. "There's no other explanation. He believed he'd killed me and he panicked. In truth I wasn't even unconscious, just too stunned to do anything except lie there like a corpse. Anyway, he rode off into the storm on a horse that was barely controllable at the best of times. Seconds later he was dead."

Sophie's hands trembled. "Oh, *mon dieu*," she breathed.

Dominic smiled ruefully at her. "When you tried to run away tonight in another thunderstorm, it was as if it was all happening again, but this time I was determined it wouldn't end the same way. I couldn't prevent Harry's death, but I could certainly prevent yours."

Sophie got up and went to him, standing on tiptoe to kiss his cheek. "I have misjudged you, *milord*. I knew there was something terrible between you and Lady Camilla, and I asked Mary. She told me Lady Camilla blamed you for letting Sir Harry die. But you didn't let him die, you behaved honorably, and I am sorry I ever thought badly of you."

"Don't credit me with the next thing to sanctity, Sophie, for I don't deserve it. Indeed I've been quite the hypocrite, wagging my finger at you and preaching about observing vows. I wanted Camilla to break her vows for me, and that is hardly the conduct of an honorable man."

Sophie smiled. "Did you wish her to be your mistress, *milord*?"

William cleared his throat uncomfortably. "You can't ask things like that, Sophie."

"I wish to know. Well, *milord*? Will you answer me?"

Dominic sipped the cognac. "The answer is no, for Camilla is far too good to be merely a mistress, Sophie. If I'd won her heart, I would have wanted her to be my wife."

"Then you were honorable, sir," Sophie replied simply.

Dominic smiled. "You're too kind."

William struggled to his feet, and looked at Dominic. "So it's still unresolved between you and Camilla?"

"And likely to remain so. I was wrong to keep the truth from her."

Sophie sighed. "But you did it for the best, Lord Ennismount, surely she will see that?"

"She feels betrayed, not only by Harry and Elizabeth, but also by me, and I suppose I'd feel the same way if I were her. The situation was impossible from the outset, and I fear I've always been destined to lose. She wouldn't leave Harry for me, and after his death I couldn't destroy her illusions about him. *Impasse*." He finished the cognac. "Anyway, that's enough reminiscing. I wanted you to know what tonight's rumpus was really about, and now you do. I wish I could offer you hope for your own future, but I can't. The Prussian match is internationally important, and that's what has to be considered."

William took Sophie's hand and pulled her closer, as if by doing so he somehow warded off the inevitable.

Dominic returned his glass to the table, and then paused. "One thing I can try to do, however, is see you're not parted until the very last moment. William, I'm sure Camilla won't hold it against you that you're Elizabeth's brother, and insist upon your early departure, especially if you swear to conduct yourself decorously. Do you give your word?"

"Of course," William replied.

"As I said earlier, gather ye rosebuds while ye may." Dominic went to the door, but Sophie hurried after him.

"*Milord!* There is something I must say to you. Something you should know about Lady Camilla."

"Oh? And what might that be?"

She glanced archly at William, and then looked at Dominic again. "I must tell you this, *milord,* even though a lady should never refer to a gentleman's, er, private life."

He was amused. "I haven't had much of a private life for years now, so I can't imagine what you're about to say."

"It concerns the serving girl you stayed with at the inn on our way here."

William was appalled. "Sophie!"

Her cheeks went a little pink, but she held her ground. "Lord Ennismount, what you do not know is that Lady Camilla was very jealous that night. She, er—what is the phrase? She bit my head off?"

"That sounds about right," Dominic murmured, smiling.

"You see, I told her she was being horrid to me because she wished she was the serving girl," Sophie explained.

William closed his eyes.

But Dominic only gave a quick laugh. "I can imagine how well she took that particular observation!"

William squirmed visibly. "Please don't say any more, Sophie," he pleaded, but she was unrepentant.

"It's all the truth," she declared, but then at last looked a little sheepish. "Have I offended you, Lord Ennismount?"

Dominic smiled and shook his head. "No, of course not, but it has to be said that Camilla had nothing to be jealous of that night. I didn't spend any time with the serving girl, I merely allowed her ladyship to draw that conclusion. It was perverse conduct on my part, but it made me feel a little better at the time, especially the following morning."

"The following . . . ?" Sophie's eyes cleared. "It was All Fools' Day! *Poisson d'avril!*"

Dominic was puzzled for a moment. "April fish? Ah, of course, that's what the French say."

Sophie lowered her eyes. "I—I merely wished you to know about it, *milord*. Lady Camilla may be angry with you now, but—"

"But nothing, Sophie. I'm afraid she'll probably stay angry with me, but thank you anyway."

"I know you think I am a foolish child, but I am not. I can see that Lady Camilla loves you as much as you love her."

William was now thoroughly embarrassed. "You've said far too much already, Sophie."

Dominic opened the door. "You're wrong about one thing, Sophie."

"I am?"

"Yes. I no longer see you as a foolish child."

"I grew up tonight, *milord*."

"Perhaps you did. Good night."

"Good night."

He crossed the entrance hall toward the dining room, where he lit a candle to take through into the conservatory. Sleep wouldn't come tonight, and he intended to pass the time at the billiard table.

Soon the lamps cast their glow over the green baize, and the ivory balls clinked together as he gathered them. Then he heard a sound outside. He glanced out, but could only see his own reflection surrounded by the thick tropical foliage. Then he heard the sound again. It was the slow clip-clop of hooves on the stone-flagged terrace. Beyond his reflection, he saw the ghostly shape of a horse. It was the roan stallion.

Slowly he opened the French windows and went out into the night. The horse was quiet now the storm was over, and it didn't sheer away as he approached. He caught the bridle and ran his hand down the animal's neck. "Steady now, boy," he murmured, bending to check it hadn't come to any obvious harm.

As he straightened he sensed someone was watching him. His gaze was drawn to an upstairs window. Camilla was silhouetted by candlelight. She looked down at him for a long moment then drew the curtains, shutting him out.

He continued to look up at the window, but then the night breeze carried a sweet sound. It was the music of the wind chimes.

Chapter 21

The house felt claustrophobic to Camilla when she awoke early the next morning. Still wounded by the previous night's shattering revelations, she didn't want to face anyone. She needed to escape into the fresh air for a while, and because it was a sunny spring day decided to go out for a walk. She put on a long-sleeved cream woolen gown and brushed her hair loose, then, with a warm cashmere shawl over her shoulders, she slipped quietly down through the house.

She hurried through the dining room to the conservatory, and there halted in dismay, for Dominic had fallen asleep in one of the chairs. The lamps were still lit above the billiard table, where his cue lay on the green baize. His hair was disheveled and he'd discarded his coat. His neckcloth was undone, as were the top buttons of his shirt, and she could see the dark hairs on his chest. He was deeply asleep, and knew nothing as she stood looking down at him.

Anger and resentment rose through her again when she thought of the two long years he'd denied her the truth about Harry. What a simpleton she'd been. His silence struck at the heart of her dignity and pride, and

she would *never* forgive him. She almost wished she
hadn't heard his scathing exchanges with Elizabeth
the night before, for now she was even being denied
her memories. She, poor fool, suspected nothing
while her husband betrayed her with her best friend.
Dominic could have spared her this delayed humilia-
tion, but he said nothing.

She'd always been ashamed of having been attracted to him, now that shame was ten times worse.
If her perfidious senses ever played Judas to her conscience again, she knew she'd despise herself forever.
She'd been at the mercy of others for too long, and
from now on intended to be entirely her own woman.
Harry no longer had any claim on her loyalty or even
her love, and two years of resounding silence had put
Dominic beyond the pale forever.

Drawing her shawl more closely around her shoulders, she moved silently past him to the French doors
on to the terrace. She opened them softly and slipped
out into the warm morning sunshine.

She found herself following the path she and Dominic had taken on the night William broke his ankle.
Daffodils bobbed by her feet, and the soft April
breeze rustled through the blossoms of the ornamental
almond trees at the edge of the Chinese garden. She
could hear the stream cascading down the hillside, but
above all she could hear the wind chimes on the
pagoda.

Pausing, she gazed up at the scarlet-and-gold tower,
with its soaring pinnacle and elegant upturned roofs.
It drew her like a magnet, and she began to walk toward it almost before she realized what was happening. This time she felt nothing as she passed the place
where they'd picnicked, no prick of conscience that

she and Dominic had slipped away and left Harry sleeping. How many times had Harry slipped away and left the wife whose unawareness was in itself a form of sleeping?

She walked on, making her way up the steep path toward the entrance of the pagoda. In spite of the dangerous state of the staircase inside, she knew she intended to climb to the very top. She didn't know why exactly, it was just something she felt compelled to do.

The pieces of broken banister still lay where they'd fallen at the time of William's accident, and the finer fragments cracked beneath her feet as she walked to the staircase. The wind chimes rang musically through the tower, their sound muffled now she was inside. It was a strangely seductive sound, luring her on toward the top of the building. She gathered her skirts and began to ascend the steps, pressing back against the wall as she reached the place where the rail had given way. A draft breathed coolly through the pagoda, and she shivered before continuing to climb.

At last she emerged on the topmost balcony, where the song of the chimes was all around her. It seemed to shimmer in the air, as if reflecting from the gilding on the chimes themselves, and it was a sound that drove her fierce new resolution to the four winds. Here, where she'd so nearly given her all to Dominic, it was impossible to deny the guilty past. Fresh tears stung her eyes as she gazed over the oriental beauty of the garden toward the stream as it tumbled down toward the valley floor.

She'd been there for several minutes before Dominic suddenly spoke to her from the top of the staircase.

"Why have you come here, Camilla?"

She whirled about with a startled gasp. He wore his coat now, but his neckcloth and shirt were still undone. He must have awoken in time to see her leave the conservatory. Too late she wished she'd glanced behind and seen him following.

He held her gaze. "Why here, Camilla?" he asked again.

"I have nothing to say to you," she whispered.

"No? I beg to disagree." He took a step toward her.

She backed instinctively away until she was pressed against the curving ornamental side of the balcony. "I don't want to speak to you, Dominic. Please leave me alone."

"I can't do that, Camilla. We have to settle this thing once and for all. I know you blame me for—"

"Of *course* I blame you!" she cried. "You left me in ignorance by allowing me to defend my mockery of a marriage! Have you any idea how I feel now, knowing Elizabeth was Harry's mistress?"

"I wanted to spare you, Camilla."

"Spare me? How can you possibly imagine I feel spared?" There was a catch in her voice as she struggled not to give in to the shuddering sobs rising in her throat.

"Then consider how you would have felt if I'd told you at the time of Harry's death! You'd have accused me of lying in order to win you for myself, just as you've always suspected I engineered that damned horse into Harry's hands. You still fear that I hoped the brute would be the death of him, so I could have you, don't you? Well? Don't you?"

She couldn't reply.

"Well, you've always been wrong on both counts. I've always told the truth about that horse, and I've never misled you for my own gain." He came nearer. "Your damned conscience has dictated everything for too long. You've been its slave ever since you kissed me right here where we're standing now, and you've succeeded in making me a slave to it as well! You're always so busy thinking of yourself you've never bothered to consider how *I* might have felt."

"You? No one betrayed you, Dominic, no one lied to you or made a fool of you!"

"All I did was protect you from hurt for as long as I could. I wanted to spare you the pain you feel now, but last night you finally heard it all. Now at last you know what a cheating blackguard Harry Summerton really was."

"And are you so morally perfect?" she whispered, her voice almost hidden by the melody of the chimes.

"Morally perfect?" He gave a bark of incredulous laughter. "I promise you there's nothing moral about the way I'm feeling right now, madam, in fact I feel very *immoral* indeed! My time has come, I fancy, for the scales have fallen from your eyes and you don't need shielding anymore. I'll begin by telling you exactly what happened when Harry died."

"I already know enough!"

"No, you don't, you don't know the half of it." He stood within inches of her, his eyes blazing with anger as he related his final conversation with Harry. He repeated it word-for-word, leaving nothing out, not even Harry's despicable offer to turn a blind eye if she were to be seduced.

Tears shone on her lashes and she blinked them furiously away. "You didn't have to tell me that," she whispered.

"Oh, yes, I do, Camilla, for it's the only way to make you understand. You've always blamed me for Harry's death, but you did so because of your own guilty conscience. You've never been able to forgive yourself—or me—because you once seriously considered committing adultery with me!"

"How dare you—?"

"Don't pretend to be outraged, Camilla, for it won't wash anymore. Making love was in your mind when you came up here with me on the day of the picnic, and if Harry hadn't called you when he did, it's what you and I would have done!"

"No!" She wouldn't admit it to him, she *wouldn't*!

"Damn you for your conscience, Camilla."

"And damn you for leaving me in ignorance all this time!"

He studied her in silence for a long moment. "I did what I thought was the right and honorable thing. You'd made your choice, you wanted Harry not me, and I respected that decision by doing all I could to make Harry worthy of your love. But it seems that in so doing I made myself *unworthy*. Well, I'm tired of being unworthy, Camilla, and I don't intend to put up with it any longer."

Was there an implied threat? "What do you mean?" she asked uneasily.

"I mean that the time has come for actions instead of words. Sweet reason doesn't seem to impress you, so maybe brute force will."

Her breath caught and she glanced past him toward the staircase. Could she escape?

He smiled. "Don't even contemplate it, Camilla, for

it will do no good. You've been wronging me for far
too long, and retribution is overdue." Suddenly he
caught her wrist and forced her so close that their
bodies touched, then he smiled down into her eyes.
"What price your conscience now, Camilla? I warned
you that if we met here a third time, I'd complete that
which was begun before. This is nemesis, but it's up
to you whether it is to be fulfillment, or a bitter struggle to the end. I am about to have you, madam, whatever your decision."

Alarm lunged through her and she tried to wrench
free. "Let me go!" she cried.

"Give in gracefully, Camilla, for that is what your
body wishes to do. You want me, and by God I want
you!"

"Let me go!" she cried again.

"Not until I've finished," he breathed, swinging her
roughly around until she was pressed against the inner
wall of the balcony. Then he took her chin between
his fingers to raise her mouth to his. It was a kiss that
allowed no quarter, nothing but complete subjection
would do. His parted lips closed fiercely over hers.

She tried to struggle, but he was too strong for her.
The kiss was relentless in its ferocity and skill. His
lips and tongue teased her senses as his fingers curled
voluptuously in her hair, and she felt his virility forcing against her like a steel bar. She didn't want to respond, but excitement began to pound needfully
through her. Her breasts tightened with irresistible desire as she felt all control slipping away. She was hun-
gry for this man's love, and had waited for what
seemed a lifetime to gratify that craving.

He gave a low laugh, a mixture of gladness and triumph as he sensed her capitulation. "My sweet, sweet Camilla . . ." he breathed, before kissing her again.

Her lips weakened against his, and she ceased to struggle. Her arms moved richly around him as she returned the kiss. She drew his tongue deep into her mouth. There was no pretense now, no nod in the direction of false conscience, just the exhilarating knowledge that in a few moments his body would invade hers. Fulfillment. She chose fulfillment.

The ribbon ties at the front of her bodice offered no resistance as he undid them, and she quivered with delight as he cupped her pink-tipped breast in his palm and rolled her nipple between his fingertips.

Kiss followed kiss, and their passion became almost frenzied as pent-up emotions and cravings were released at last. His arousal throbbed against her now, and her fingers shook as she slid her hand down to enclose it through the silk of his trousers. His breath caught with pleasure as she caressed the iron-hard shaft that beat just for her.

He bent his head to draw her flushed nipple into his mouth, and she gasped as he slid his tongue against it, then he found her mouth again, bruising her lips with the force of his desire. Slowly he pulled her gown up in order to slide his hand against the warmth of her naked thigh.

She was ready to receive him now, ready to savor the penetration she'd refused to admit wanting. Their lips still seared together as he undid his trousers buttons to free the pounding manhood springing from his loins.

Only then did he tear his lips from hers to gaze into her eyes. "You're mine, Camilla, and you always have been. Deny it now if you can." He spoke softy as he lifted her gently from her feet to gain final entry.

She clung to him, wrapping her legs around his hips as at last he pushed slowly into her. She gave a cry of ecstasy before his lips devoured her again. She was impaled upon him. A glory of voluptuous emotion seized her in wave after wave of erotic joy, and she felt as if the blood was turning to fire in her veins as he began to thrust. Tears stung her eyes and consciousness itself threatened to desert her as their passion dissolved into paroxysms of shuddering elation. They became one, their hearts beating in union as the pulsing excitement transported them. They were weightless, floating on a sea of exquisite joy.

The ecstasy was slow to fade, leaving them warm and sated, and when he spoke several minutes later, he was still deep inside her. "All this pleasure and love could have been ours a long time ago."

"I know. Forgive me, forgive me . . ." Tears stung her eyes as she covered his face with kisses.

"Love always forgives."

"I'm so ashamed. I punished you for everything."

"We punished each other, fools that we are," he murmured, putting his lips to the pulse at her throat.

She arched toward him, anxious to prolong the final moments of union. Her whole body ached with love for him, and she was crying softly as their lips met again before he lowered her gently to her feet.

They were two once more, but stood locked in a long embrace. At last they drew properly apart, and he tenderly retied the ribbons on her bodice before putting his hand to her chin and tilting her face toward him. "I love you, Camilla, I've always loved you, and I always will."

"And I've always loved you," she confessed. "Deep inside I knew it before I married Harry, and now I wish I'd had the courage to admit it before it was too late."

"For me it really began that day in Hyde Park."

She nodded. "I—I didn't know what to do, except try not to be alone with you again. I'd promised my hand to Harry, you see, and a promise such as that should be . . ."

"Sacrosanct?"

"Yes."

"They should also be made from the heart, Camilla, and your heart wasn't really in it when you made your marriage vows. Oh, you loved Harry, but it wasn't with the depth and ferocity of the feelings you had for me. I know how you felt, because I felt the same. We were made for each other, and if we've been kept apart until now, by God I mean to make up for it from this moment on."

She blinked back more tears. "So much wasted time," she whispered, her voice mingling with the music of the chimes as the breeze played around the pagoda.

"Time means everything, and not just to us," he said.

She looked at him. "Sophie and William?"

"Yes. I, er, took a small liberty last night. I told them I was sure you'd permit William to stay here, provided he promised to behave with absolute discretion. Was I right to think you'd agree?"

"Of course. They're very much in love and know they must soon part forever."

"Gather ye rosebuds while ye may," he murmured.

She smiled and murmured the whole quotation. "Gather ye rosebuds while ye may, Old Time is still a-flying: And this same flower that smiles to-day, To-morrow will be dying."

Chapter 22

Over the following days Sophie and William stole every moment they could to be together before being parted forever. Camilla felt desperately sorry for them, especially now that she was so very happy herself. After her passionate surrender in the pagoda, she gladly gave herself to Dominic every night, and quite often during the day as well.

They were discreet, of course, but when they were alone, they gave their newly acknowledged passion its long-overdue liberty. The past was erased more and more with each night they spent in each other's arms, and the anguish she felt on learning about Harry and Elizabeth was soon an almost forgotten pain. Harry's infidelity served as a balm to her conscience, erasing the guilt that had tormented her for so long. It also clarified something she hardly realized had begun to cast a shadow over her existence, and that was her increasingly equivocal feelings toward Summerton Park itself.

The house she once loved so much was suddenly no longer a home. It was Harry's home, for centuries the country seat of his family, and now it was alien to her. She could no longer bring herself to sleep in the bed she'd shared with him, but went to Dominic's room at night, and when she looked at the priceless collection of chinoiserie, she felt only indifference. She hadn't realized how her conscience had turned her into a prisoner, or how the house, with all its memories, had become her jail. But now her sentence was over, the doors had been flung open, and she intended to walk through to freedom. The only way was to sell the house, and this she privately decided to do as soon as Sophie and William's brief interlude of happiness was brought to an end.

The illicit young lovers were out riding in the park when a traveling carriage bowled toward the house three days after Elizabeth's disgraced departure. Camilla saw it approaching and her spirits sank, for somehow she felt sure it heralded the final moments of happiness for the czar's ward and her young English lord. But as the vehicle drew to a standstill and the coat of arms on its door was revealed, Camilla realized it belonged to Elizabeth's husband, George. He was alone, and looked a little weary as he alighted.

It was another beautiful spring day, sunny, warm, and clear, the sort of day nothing should ever be allowed to blight, but it seemed the sun went behind a cloud as he was admitted. Camilla and Dominic waited in the drawing room as he was conducted up the staircase. She sat in a fireside chair, her hands clasped uneasily in her lap, and Dominic stood by a window, his back to the rest of the room.

Hawkins announced the visitor. "Sir George Oxforth."

George came in, his quick glance encompassing the room's two occupants. He waited until the butler had closed the door again, and then turned to Camilla.

"Elizabeth told me everything," he said without pre-amble. "When she arrived in London she came straight to me to confess about her affair with Harry. I'm so very sorry, Camilla. I don't know what else to say."

She smiled. "You have nothing to apologize for, George."

"I should have stopped her infidelities years ago. For what it's worth, she's desperately sorry about the whole business. Falling out with you has made her study herself properly for the first time. She doesn't like what she sees. Nor do I, but I still love her," he added under his breath.

Dominic turned. "We can't help falling in love, George."

"Don't I know it. I've tried to remain immune to Elizabeth's liaisons, but it's impossible. Learning about Harry was the final straw, and I told her so. I said we should separate, but she begged me to recon-sider. She swears she'll be a true wife from now on."

"Do you believe her?" Dominic asked dryly.

George shrugged. "I don't know. All I can say is I've never seen her so low and broken before. Maybe she means it, but she's always been such a consum-mate actress that it's impossible to tell."

Camilla looked at him. "I think you can believe her, George," she said after a moment.

"Why do you say that?"

"Because I've always believed that by the time she realized your worth, it would be almost too late. I don't know if it's too late for you or not, but I do know that when she left here no one even spoke to her. In one fell swoop she'd lost the regard of her brother and her oldest friend, and who did she run to? You."

He smiled bitterly. "Yes, good old dependable boring George."

"You say you still love her. If that's so you must give her one last chance. For your own sake, if not for hers."

He looked quizzically at her. "Why are you pleading on her behalf? After what's happened, I'd have thought you'd be the last person on earth to speak up for her. You owe her nothing."

"On the contrary, George, I owe her a great deal. Oh, don't think I'm an angel, for I'm far from that. Truth to tell, I'm too content now to bear any grudges." She smiled at Dominic.

George glanced at them both. "So that's the way of it, eh? About damned time, too. I could have told you fifteen years ago that the wrong man was getting the bride. There have been times over the past two years when I could gladly have knocked your silly heads together for continuing that pointless feud. Still, better late than never. Anyway, that's by the by, but you aren't the ones I've really come to see. Where are Mlle Arenburg and William?"

Camilla was immediately anxious. "You have news?"

"I do indeed."

"Oh, I can hardly bear it. They're so desperately in love, you see." Tears filled Camilla's eyes as she thought of the terrible distress the forced parting was going to cause.

"I know they are. I said that Elizabeth told me everything, and so she did, including how despicably cruel she was to Mlle Arenburg simply because she was the cause of Dominic's presence here. Camilla, I'm afraid that my wife was originally anxious to keep you buried away here in the country, because that meant you would not encounter Dominic, who knew the full truth about her liaison with Harry. Then you went to London anyway, and she was in a lather because he was in town as well. It was her worst nightmare when you actually spoke to him at Carlton House, but it seemed to pass off without event and she relaxed again. Then she found out he was to come here and actually stay beneath this roof, and she became quite distraught. She saw it all as Mlle Arenburg's fault, for if it were not for her, you and Dominic would not have been thrust together like this. It didn't suit her to blame William, and it certainly didn't suit her to blame herself for having such a dark and despicable secret to hide. However, she has atoned a little now, as you'll realize when I tell you what's happened over the past day or so." He paused for dramatic effect. "To begin with, Mlle Arenburg's match with Prince Ludwig is off."

Camilla gasped, and Dominic's lips parted in surprise. "Off, did you say?" he repeated.

"Yes." George was enjoying breaking such astonishing news.

Dominic searched his face. "What's happened, George?"

"Prince Ludwig is in disgrace." George glanced longingly toward a decanter on a nearby table. "Must I die of thirst before you offer me refreshment?"

"Forgive me." Dominic hastened to a small table to pour him a liberal measure from the decanter of cognac standing on it.

George accepted the glass. "Now, where was I? Oh,

yes. Prince Ludwig. Well, he duly arrived with the Grand Duchess Catherine, and was hauled along to Carlton House to be presented to Prinny. However, Princess Charlotte was there as well, and since Ludwig is desperately handsome, she temporarily forgot her betrothal to the Prince of Orange in order to make sheep's eyes at the Prince of Prussia instead! They said Ludwig saw a chance of winning the future Queen of England, and made the most of his opportunity."

Camilla's lips parted. "Made the most? What are you saying?"

"That foolish Charlotte very nearly surrendered her all in a closet! Her ladies realized what was happening and interrupted the pair, but the princess's gown was in some disarray. This isn't for onward transmission of course, and has been hushed up with a vengeance."

"Of course. You have our word," Dominic reassured him.

"I'll hold you to that," George replied. "Prinny's beside himself with rage, as you can imagine, and Ludwig has already been kicked back across the Channel. Charlotte has been dispatched to cool her heels at Windsor, where her shocked aunts are no doubt making her life wretched. The Grand Duchess Catherine wanted to stir up trouble in Charlotte's betrothal, which doesn't suit Russia, but she didn't envisage Ludwig's involvement. Anyway, the Orange match may be a little rocky, but it still holds good, which is more than can be said for the Prussian match. The grand duchess still hoped to rescue it, but the Russian ambassador is totally opposed and threatened to inform the czar of Ludwig's manifest unsuitability. No one knows whether or not the ambassador would carry out such a threat, but he might, and apart from that there was word from St. Petersburg that Mlle Arenburg is no longer the czar's only child—" George broke off hastily, and glanced at Camilla.

Dominic smiled. "It's all right, George, Camilla knows Mlle Arenburg is the czar's daughter."

George relaxed. "Well, there is now an illegitimate son as well, and, needless to say, said son has taken up the czar's attention. It's no longer of any particular consequence to Alexander whether or not his daughter marries royalty. The grand duchess isn't a fool and knows when it is best to bow out gracefully from any situation. The Prussian match has therefore been allowed to expire."

Camilla was smiling broadly now. "So there's absolutely no doubt that Sophie no longer has to marry Prince Ludwig?"

"None whatsoever."

Her eyes shone delightedly. "Oh, I'm so glad!" But then she remembered something. "You said Elizabeth had atoned?"

"Ah, yes, I was just coming to that." George took a sip of the cognac. "You see, the grand duchess was smarting a little that the czar would be displeased because her choice for Mlle Arenburg had proved so shabby, and it occurred to Elizabeth that there was an excellent way for the grand duchess to save face. She therefore told her about Mlle Arenburg being head-over-heels in love with William."

Camilla's eyes widened. "Wasn't that a little risky?"

"No, because Elizabeth rightly perceived that the grand duchess would seize upon it as an excellent reason to give to the czar for wishing to dispense with the Prussian match. No mention need be made of Prince Ludwig's gross misconduct and disgrace, the czar need only be told that his favorite sister had elected to support the course of true love. The Russian ambassador has been consulted, and is in favor of this new match. Word has been sent to St. Petersburg, but the czar's consent is only a matter of course. He's certain to accept his sister's new suggestion because as the future Earl, nay, Duke of Highnam, William is actually a tolerable match for Mlle Arenburg, who is, after all, now only the lesser of the two imperial byblows, if you'll excuse the rather vulgar expression."

But Camilla wasn't concerned about the possible vulgarity of the expression, she was too startled by something else he'd said. "Did you say *Duke* of Highnam? I thought a marquessate was the expected thing."

"It was, but the grand duchess feels a dukedom would be more appropriate. She has let Prinny know she is sure the czar would be personally very pleased if that were to be the case, and Prinny will do it, you may be sure of that. He's walking on eggshells in order not to offend the czar, and has been making himself ill over this whole Arenburg debacle. He dreaded the czar discovering what happened at the ball, and sees this new development as an ideal solution. All can now be safely swept under the royal carpet, if you see what I mean."

"So the prince won't be telling tales on William to his father?" Camilla asked, hardly daring to believe all she was hearing.

"Eh? Good God, no. Prinny's only too eager to let these particular bygones remain bygones. As for old Highnam, he won't be able to believe his luck when he hears, and is certainly not likely to carry out any threat concerning William's present betrothal to Alice Penshill. Loyalty to one's old friends is one thing, becoming a duke quite another. You may count upon it, William is going to be welcomed with open arms and congratulated not disinherited for his liaison with Mlle Arenburg." George took a long breath and beamed at them both. "*Ergo,* our troublesome young lovers can now return to London whenever they wish, and the wedding they both long for will follow in due course."

Camilla suddenly felt close to tears. "I—I can hardly believe it. Oh, I wish they'd return from their ride so we can tell them."

Dominic glanced from the window again. "Your wish is granted, for they're coming now." He smiled. "They've seen George's carriage, and fear the worst."

She hurried to join him. Sophie and William had reined in on seeing the carriage, and their dismay was almost palpable. William leaned across to put a comforting hand over that of his love, and Sophie's little face was full of misery. Then they slowly continued to ride toward the house.

As they passed out of sight, Dominic's fingers closed over Camilla's. "So Sophie's rosebud-gathering wasn't such a thorny business after all, hmm?"

"No, and I couldn't be more glad."

He looked at her. "Well, they'll always gather rosebuds now, my darling. And so will we." He hesitated. "Leave this place, Camilla, in fact, sell up and start everything anew."

"I have already decided to do that. This isn't my home anymore, it's still Harry's, and I want none of it."

Suddenly he drew her fingertips passionately to his lips. "Come to me. It's where you belong."

Her heart stopped. "Come to you?"

"As my wife. You were always meant to be Countess of Ennismount, and we've waited far too long. Say you'll marry me, Camilla."

Joy sang magnificently through her. "Yes," she whispered. "Oh, yes, I will."

Ignoring George, he pulled her into his arms and kissed her fiercely on the lips, crushing her to him as if she were his other self. Which she was.

George smiled, and then turned to raise his glass to Harry's portrait. "You weren't properly buried two years ago, but you are now, you old bastard. Good riddance to you at last," he murmured cordially.